LADY GUNSMITH

5

The Portrait of Gavin Doyle

LADY GUNSMITH

5

The Portrait of Gavin Doyle

J.R. Roberts

SPEAKING VOLUMES, LLC
NAPLES, FLORIDA
2018

The Portrait of Gavin Doyle

ISBN 978-1-62815-788-8

PART ONE

PORTRAIT

Chapter One

Roxy Doyle did not normally read newspapers, for two reasons: She rarely had time, and she believed very little of what she read, especially the things about her mentor, Clint Adams, and herself.

But she was sitting alone in a small café in the town of Jerome, Wyoming. It was the type of place she liked to patronize, with very few tables and even fewer customers. The food was edible, which was all she ever required. She rarely ate for enjoyment, rather she consumed food as fuel to keep herself going.

But on the table next to her someone had left a copy of the *Arizona Sun*, which was published out of Flagstaff. She decided to reach over and grab it, and while away the time reading while she ate her eggs.

The front page had two interesting stories, both of which were several weeks old. Earlier in the month Sheriff Pat Garrett had apparently finally tracked down Billy the Kid in New Mexico, shot and killed him. That was the kind of story Roxy was never sure she could believe. How many times had she read that Clint Adams had been killed, or that her father, famed bounty hunter Gavin Doyle had been killed only to discover they hadn't?

The second story occurred about a week after the Billy the Kid story. Sitting Bull, chief of the Lakota Sioux Nation, had surrendered and was imprisoned in Fort Yates, in South

Dakota, near the Standing Rock Indian Reservation. While Sitting Bull had no direct connection to Custer's defeat at Little Big Horn, it was said that his visions inspired the actions of Crazy Horse.

This was where Roxy's perusal of a newspaper usually stopped, but since she had time on her hands she began turning the pages. By the time she finished her breakfast and washed it down with a last cup of coffee she had come to a page that was filled with odd photos. She quickly realized that they were photos of pictures of people, not the people themselves. Finding that odd, she began to study them. When she came to one in particular, her heart stopped.

The photos were not large, and they were out of focus. Also, it had been well over a dozen years, since she had last seen her father. But she thought that one of the photos resembled him. Of course, it was an older version, and was taken from the waist up. But there was something about the set of his jaw, and his eyes, that made Roxy's heart beat faster.

Was this her father? The face was covered by a beard and even in the black-and-white photo she could tell the beard was grey. But there was also something in the set of his shoulders . . .

She read the entire story, which had to do with a photography studio located in Santa Fe, New Mexico. Apparently, the photos had been taken by someone named Mathew Brady, and the studio was his.

Roxy had been riding rather aimlessly in the weeks since leaving Denver, Colorado. She had spent some time with a traveling circus, because of a rumor her father might be there.

He wasn't, and since then she'd heard no other rumors. She was actually starting to wonder if the rumors were going to fade after all so many years of looking, but this wasn't exactly a rumor.

She decided to take the newspaper outside into the sunlight to take a better look at the photo. If she still felt that it might be her father, then a ride to Santa Fe was in order. Since Flagstaff, where the newspaper was based, was on the way, she could also stop in at the office of the *Sun* and see what they could tell her.

At least she would once again have a direction.

***

"You sure she's in there?" Hank Beldon asked.

"I told you," Ed Lane said, "I seen her in there for two mornings. This is the place."

"Ain't nobody come in or out in an hour," Davey Lane, Ed's brother, complained.

"Then she's probably in there alone," Sonny Franklin said. "Why don't we go in and get 'er?"

"No, we're gonna wait out here," Ed Lane said. "Just as she comes out the sun's gonna be in her eyes."

"You sure she's who you say she is, Ed?" his brother asked.

"Lady Gunsmith, Davey," Ed said, annoyed. "I knows what I'm talkin' about. You seen 'er, all that red hair, and that gun. It's her!"

"This is gonna be somethin'," Franklin said.

"Yeah, it is," Ed Lane said, "it's gonna be somethin' for sure."

***

Roxy paid her bill and headed for the door. The sun was shining brightly and she hesitated. Clint Adams had explained to her that brilliant sunlight was not her friend. It would either blind her, or spotlight her, like she was on stage. So she paused just inside the door, and in that moment a cloud passed in front of the sun and she saw the four men.

Chapter Two

Just what she needed.

"There's a back way," the waiter told her, pointing. "Through the kitchen."

"Thanks," she said, "but if I get that reputation, they'll be waiting for me outside every door the rest of my life."

"I could go out the back and get the sheriff," he offered. He was not a young man, but he was young enough to be enamored of her, and he didn't want to see her get shot.

"Why don't you go into the kitchen," she suggested, "just in case some lead comes flying through the window."

"A-all right."

She still had the newspaper in her left hand, and now she folded it, tucked it into her belt. There was a shaft of bright sunlight on the door again. She was fairly certain that, if she stepped out directly into it, they'd start firing immediately, while she was blinded. But right at that moment another cloud passed by, and she seized the moment to stop.

***

"Goddamn clouds!" Ed Lane swore.

"It's a beautiful day," Davey said, frowning. He was not the brightest of the two brothers, even though he was the oldest. "The clouds look like big pillows."

"And they're blockin' the sun," Ed said. "We need the sun to get in her eyes."

"It's passin', Ed," Hank Beldon said. "Take it easy."

But just as he said it another big, white, puffy cloud passed in front of the sun, and Lady Gunsmith came out of the café.

"Crap!" Ed Lane swore, and grabbed for his gun.

***

One of Clint Adams' first lessons to Roxy was, never grab for your gun. You draw it in a smooth, easy motion. Most men who grab at their weapons often drop it as they yank it from their holster, or fired it prematurely, sometimes shooting themselves in the foot.

"Also, as your reputation grows," he explained, "the moves against you will be herky-jerky, panicked moves. So don't ever rush. You're naturally faster than anyone else, but you also need to be accurate."

She saw one of the men suddenly grab for his gun. The other three, totally unprepared, tried to follow. Grabbing, and panicked.

She drew her gun in one easy, fluid motion.

***

The waiter had not gone into the kitchen. In fact, the cook had come out of the kitchen, and they were both taking their lives in their hands by watching from the window. But there was really no danger, because the Lady Gunsmith did not allow any of the four men to get off a shot.

She shot the first one dead center in the chest, causing him to drop immediately, then turned her attention to the others.

"*Ah, dios mio,*" the Mexican cook said, his eyes popping out of his head.

"You said it, Carlos," the waiter said. "She's really somethin'."

As they watched she calmly shot each of the other three men, even before they could remove their guns from their holsters. In what seemed like a second, all four men were lying on the ground, lifeless.

"Perhaps we should send for the sheriff," Carlos suggested.

"Not to worry," the waiter said. "Here he comes, and he don't look happy."

***

"This is just what I was afraid of when you came to town!" the lawman snapped.

"Hey," she said, ejecting the spent shells and replacing them, "I was just havin' a quiet breakfast. They were waiting for me when I came out. Ask the waiter."

"She's right, Sheriff," the waiter called from the door.

"Shut up, Clarence," the fiftyish lawman said. "I been sheriff here a long time, Doyle, and I don't allow this. You gotta leave."

"That's just what I was planning on doing, Sheriff," she said, walking to her horse. "You sure you don't need me to testify?"

"I just need you to ride out," he said. "I ain't stupid. I know what happened here, but I also know if you wasn't in town, this wouldn'ta happened, at all."

"You're probably right about that, Sheriff," Roxy said, mounting up.

She rode out of town without another word.

The waiter, Clarence, came out and stared after her, mournfully.

"Clarence!" the lawman snapped.

"Yessir?"

"Get Carlos to help you move these bodies," the sheriff said. "You ain't gonna get no business with them lyin' there."

Chapter Three

Jerome to Flagstaff was roughly a two day ride.

If she'd had a good horse she would have pushed it to a day-and-a-half, but she was riding a worn out steel dust she had bought with the money won in a sharpshooting contest some time back. And since she'd paid a pretty penny, she was determined to ride him until he couldn't walk, anymore. Not that she intended to ride him into the ground . . . but close.

So she camped overnight, once again gazing at the photo in the newspaper, but the half moon and campfire did nothing to make it any clearer. If, indeed, that had been Gavin Doyle, sitting for a portrait, somebody was going to have to tell her.

She laid on her back with the gun by her and stared at the sky. It was odd that, in all the years of searching for him, she had never thought of her father as having gotten older. She often wondered if he would recognize her, and she him, but not because of what the passing of time might have done to them, physically. For her it was more mental. Would she know him, what would she say to him, what questions would she demand answers for?

But before the questions she was going to have to recognize him and know for sure it was him. If, indeed, this portrait photograph in the newspaper was how he looked now, it would be a big help if and when she found him.

But the hard part was still finding him.

***

When she woke in the morning she made a pot of coffee but didn't bother with anything to eat. She had two cups, then poured the rest of it over the fire to douse it. That done she saddled the weary steel dust and mounted up.

"Don't worry, boy," she said. "When we get to Flagstaff I'll have you put out to pasture . . . if I can find somebody who will trade."

***

She made Flagstaff by midday.

It was obviously a growing community. She passed rows of houses on the outskirts; the main street was very wide and filled with business storefronts.

She found the office of the *Arizona Sun* right on the main street. She dismounted, tied her horse to a hitching post and went inside, carrying the newspaper.

The sound of the printing press was deafening. The young man running it noticed her right away and stopped what he was doing to stare. Abruptly, the press stopped and it was quiet.

That brought another, older man out from a back office. Not so old, though, just in his 30's. The boy at the press was still wet behind the ears—which were huge.

"Danny, what the hell—that issue is not gonna get itself printed!"

"Yessir."

He started the press again and the man looked at Roxy.

"Can I help you?" he shouted.

"Can we talk someplace quieter?" she called back.

He nodded. "Come into my office."

He led her to a messy office. Once they were inside and the door was closed, it was a lot quieter.

"That's better," she said.

"The price we pay for bein' newspapermen, I think. I'll probably be deaf by the time I'm forty. I'm Zack Eldridge, the editor and publisher of the *Sun*. What can I do for you, Miss?"

"I need to know," she said, handing him the issue she was holding, "who put this story in your paper."

He looked down at it. She had folded it to the page of photos.

"Oh, that," Eldridge said. "Why, that ain't even a story, it's more of an advertisement for a photography gallery in Santa Fe."

"Did this Mathew Brady send it to you?"

"Not Brady himself," the man said, "but an assistant. Uh, you know who Brady is, don't you?"

"Afraid not," she said. "I don't read newspapers very much."

"Mr. Brady is the most famous photographer in the country," the man said. "He made his reputation photographing battlefields during the war."

"Who wants to see that?" she asked, puzzled. "A bunch of dead bodies?"

"Well, apparently a lot of people do," Eldridge said, handing the paper back. "That issue's a few weeks old."

"I know," she said, "but I just saw it yesterday morning. I'm on my way to Santa Fe, but I thought I'd check in with you since I was passing by."

"I can't tell you much," Eldridge said. "The assistant sent us a collection of Brady's work and paid to have them printed."

"Do you have his name?"

"Oh, sure," he said. "I got it right here." He turned to a file cabinet, reached into the top drawer and came out with a folder. He took a piece of paper out and read it. "His name's Sam Woodruff."

"You got an address for him?"

"Just the Brady Gallery, Santa Fe, New Mexico." He put the folder back. "My guess is you won't be able to miss it."

"Well . . . thank you."

"Is there anything I can do for you?" he asked. "Why the interest, if I may ask."

"There's nothing else you can do for me," she said, turning to leave, "and no, you may not."

Chapter Four

She wasn't too tired to continue on to New Mexico, but the horse was. Plus, she was hungry. When she left the newspaper office the boy at the press stared at her all the way to the door, then looked out the window when she got outside. She grabbed her horse's reins and started walking with it up the street.

She didn't notice the stares. She had learned to accept them and had taught herself the difference between what she got from men and what came from women. She also instinctively knew when a man was looking at her for more reasons than just her looks. She wasn't getting that feeling from anyone she passed—yet.

She kept walking until she came to what she wanted—a saloon. After tying off the horse again she went inside. Midday, the place wasn't crowded, which suited her. Crowded saloons usually had a few idiots in them, and that was where the trouble came from.

"Help ya, young lady?" the bartender asked. The man was in his late 50's, so she let the "young lady" comment slide.

"Beer," she said, "and do you have anything to eat?"

"Sorry, we don't serve food, but there's a cantina about two blocks up."

"Cantina? Or café?"

"No, it's a cantina, all right. Serves whiskey and beer and really good Mexican food.

She sipped the beer, found it cold and refreshing.

"Is their beer as good as this?" she asked.

"Hell, no," he said, "we got the best beer in town. But like I said, they got the best Mexican food."

"Much obliged," she said. "I'll finish this and then mosey on down there."

"And if you eat somethin' real spicy," the man said, "come on back and I'll give ya one on the house."

"You got a deal," she said.

He leaned forward and kept his voice down.

"Just don't tell nobody about it," he said. "I only give free beers to pretty ladies."

He was smiling, and it wasn't in the least bit a leering or bawdy smile. He was just being a nice guy. She didn't run into too many of them, these days.

"What's your name?"

"Cal."

"Well, thanks, Cal," she said. "My lips'll be sealed. I promise."

***

Cal was right about the food in the cantina. A black-haired girl in a peasant blouse welcomed Roxy in, allowed her to pick whatever table she liked, as the place was empty.

"The bartender at the saloon down the street says you have the best Mexican food in town," she said, seating herself at a back table.

"*Si, si*," the woman said, "the best."

"Then bring me some."

The woman frowned. She was in her forties, build solidly, just starting to show her age, but probably a real beauty when she was younger.

"What would you like, *Senorita*?" she asked.

"Anything," Roxy said. "Just bring me what's good."

"*Si, Senorita*," the woman said, smiling and taking some years off, returning her face to the beauty of her younger years, "*muy bien.*"

Roxy had never been to Mexico and hadn't eaten very much Mexican food in her life—especially not in her youth in Utah. There wasn't much Mexican food in Mormon communities.

The waitress brought a big plate of rice and beans, and then some meat wrapped in tortillas which she said were *enchiladas*. Then she brought out another plate with meat in crispy tortillas she told Roxy they were *tacos*. Roxy had heard of them but had never tasted any. She took one bite of an *enchilada* and the flavors exploded in her mouth. The same with the *tacos*, so she proceeded to chow down on everything the woman had brought her, washing it down with beer that certainly was not as good as the one in the saloon. But it served its purpose, here.

When she was finished she wiped her mouth on a red cloth napkin and finished the mug of lukewarm beer.

"More?" the woman asked.

"No," Roxy said, "no more food, or beer. That was very good."

"*Gracias.*"

"Do you own this place?"

"*Si,*" she said, "with my husband, *Roberto*. He is also the cook."

"Well, tell him this was the best meal I've had in a long time."

She stood up.

"Come back again, *por favor*," the woman said.

"I would, but I'm just passing through, so I won't be able to," Roxy said. "But thank you . . ."

"Pilar," the woman said, "my name is Pilar."

"Thank you, Pilar."

As Roxy left, Pilar's husband came out of the kitchen to watch.

"*Muy bonita*, eh?" he said.

She slapped him on the arm and said, "Go back to the kitchen!"

"She is not as beautiful as you, my sweet," he said, touching her face.

"Go," she said, "go back to work."

He was a silly man, but she loved him . . . and, oh he could cook!

Chapter Five

The streets were busy at midday, so she was getting more long looks as she walked her horse along, looking for a livery stable. She finally asked a young boy where the closest stable was, and he directed her to one that would also have horses to trade or sell.

The stable was off the main street, at the end of a long side street. It was isolated from the center of town hubbub.

She walked her horse in and looked around. It was a good size, with horses in most of the stalls, and she had spotted a corral out back.

"Help ya?" a man asked, coming from the back, wiping his hands on a rag. His age was hard to tell from the dirt on his face, but he stood tall and straight.

"I'm looking for a new horse," she said. "But I need to trade, not buy."

"For that steel dust?" he asked.

She nodded.

"What's wrong with him?"

"He's tired," she said. "I can't use a tired horse."

The man stepped forward and took the time to examine the horse, running his hands along his legs and flanks.

"He seems sound," the man said. "What is he, about five or six?"

"You'd know better than me," she said.

He looked at the animal's teeth.

"Yep, about five or six," he said.

"You got something we could trade?" she asked.

"What are ya lookin' for?"

"Just a sound animal that'll get me where I'm going."

"And where's that?"

"Santa Fe."

"I got a couple of mares and an older gelding I could trade for. You wanna see 'em?"

"Which would be better for what I need?"

"Well, they're all sound, but also older than this one. I got an eight-year old mare I can trade straight up for."

It didn't sound like a fair trade to her, but the animal would get her to Santa Fe and wouldn't die of old age along the way.

"I'll take her," she said. "Can you saddle her for me?"

"Don't you wanna take a look first?"

"I passed a small saloon along the way," she said. "I'll get a beer there and then come back. If I think you're cheating me I'll let you know."

He studied her, then said, "Okay, fair enough. I'll have her ready to travel in half an hour."

Much obliged.

She didn't have anything in the saddlebags that she couldn't leave behind, so all she took when she left was her rifle.

***

19

Roxy had a beer in the quiet interior of the small saloon, pleased to find herself not the center of attention for any drunks.

When she got back to the livery she walked in, looked around the empty interior, didn't see either her horse or the saddle mare. She was about to shout for the hostler when the livery doors closed behind her. Since it was light outside the interior wasn't completely dark, as some shafts of light were coming in between boards of the walls.

As she turned to look behind her someone lit a lamp, and she saw two men standing there. In front of her the hostler appeared holding the lamp and wearing a sick smile.

"What's going on?" she asked. "I don't have any money. If I had, I would've bought a better horse."

"Oh, don't worry," the man said. "You'll get yer horse. We just thought you might wanna have some fun first."

She turned sideways so she could look at the men behind her and the one in front of her at the same time. One of the two behind was leering, but the other had a look of concern on his face.

"Wait a minute—" he said, and she knew that he had recognized her.

"You fellas don't want to do this," she said.

"Oh yeah, we do," the hostler said. He was still filthy, but through the grime she could now see he was in his 40's, like the other two. "How many chances are we gonna get to have fun with a gal like you?"

"Only one," she said. "After this, none of you will be able to."

"Why not?" the second man asked.

"Because you'll all be dead."

The hostler showed her his other hand, which held a gun. The two men behind her were wearing holstered pistols.

"You think we're afraid of your little ol' gun?" the hostler asked.

"Andy," the third man said, speaking for the first time, "I don't think this is a good idea."

"Why not?" Andy, the hostler, asked.

"Because I don't think it's a good idea to try and rape Lady Gunsmith . . . do you?"

Chapter Six

"Whataya talkin', Tom?" Andy said.

"I'm tellin' ya," the other man said. "The red hair, the gun, that blue thing in her hat . . . this is Lady Gunsmith."

Andy scowled. "Ain't no such person."

"Let's rape 'er!" the other man shouted.

"Come on," Roxy invited, "try it." She looked at Andy. "I'll kill you first, since this was your idea."

"That's right," said Tom. "It was all his idea."

"Shaddap!" Andy said. "You ain't no Lady Gunsmith."

"It doesn't matter who I am," she said. "I'm not about to let you three slobs rape me, so make your move."

"Go ahead, Andy," Tom said. "Try 'er."

"I'll try 'er," the third man said. "I'll try ta rape 'er."

"Don't do it, Ricky," Tom said. "She'll kill you."

Ricky's leer widened. "It'll be worth it."

He started for her but didn't go for his gun. But she felt she had no choice. There were three of them, and even if none of them went for their guns, she wasn't going to let them put their hands on her.

She drew and fired, hitting Ricky in the crotch.

"Owwwwww," he howled, falling to his knees.

As she turned, Andy was bringing his gun up, so she shot him in the chest. He fell onto his back, dead before he hit the ground.

She turned to Tom.

"Whoa, whoa!" he said, putting his hands up. "I ain't goin' for my gun."

"Take it out with two fingers and toss it away," she told him.

"Yes, Ma'am." He did as he was told.

"Now," she said, "you're gonna saddle the best horse in the corral for me."

"The best horse Andy has is right here," Tom said, "in that stall." He pointed to the grey backside in one of the stalls.

"That gray?"

"That's the one."

"Where's my saddle?"

"In Andy's back room."

"Then saddle it!"

"Yes, Ma'am."

He ran to the back room to fetch the saddle, while she kept him covered.

***

When the big gray was saddled and ready to go she told Tom, "Move that body so I don't have to ride around him."

Tom dragged Ricky out of the way. He wasn't dead, but it wouldn't be long before he bled to death.

"Can I get him to a doc?"

"After I leave," she said, "you can do whatever you damn well please." She mounted up. "Although I should kill you both, just to finish the job."

"No, no," he said, putting his hands out to her in a pleading gesture, "you don't gotta do that."

"Have you fellas raped a lot of women who ride through town?" she asked.

"Well . . . some."

"Are you gonna do it anymore?"

"No, Ma'am!" he swore. "It was usually Andy's idea, and he's dead, so . . ."

"And what are you going to tell the sheriff about this?" she asked.

"I'll just tell 'im what happened," he said. "I sure will, Ma'am."

"If I find a posse after me," she said, "you're a dead man. And I'll make what I did to Ricky, there, look like a love pat. Do you understand?"

"Yes, Ma'am."

She looked around at the dead man, the bleeding man, and Tom.

"Are there any more like you in town?" she asked.

"Um, you mean—"

"Rapists!"

"Oh, no, Ma'am," Tom said, "we be the only, uh, rapists in Flagstaff."

She shook her head, wondering if leaving him alive was a good idea. But then she got another one.

***

Before leaving out of town, she rode back to the office of the *Arizona Sun*. The printing press was still going, but she walked past it, directly to the office of Zack Eldridge, the editor.

As she entered without knocking, he looked up from his desk.

"You're back!" he said. "More questions?"

"No," she said. "I've got a story for you, but you're going to have to relay it to the sheriff."

"A story? About what?"

"About three rapists in this town who made a bad decision," she said.

"Wait." He hastily picked up a pencil and a notebook. "Okay, go!"

Chapter Seven

Santa Fe, N.M.

Santa Fe spread out in front of her as she approached it on her new horse. The gray she was riding was a sturdy animal, and wasn't showing any sign of fatigue, even though she had pushed him.

As she rode through the streets of the town she saw there were many galleries in between the usual store fronts, cantinas, and hotels. It might take a while to find the one she wanted. What was it? Oh, yes, the Mathew Brady gallery.

Since she had no idea where it was located, she simply stopped at a random hotel, dismounted and went inside to get herself a room. There was no great rush, not after all these years of searching. The gallery wasn't going anywhere.

After she'd secured a room she asked the clerk, "Do you know where a Mathew Brady Gallery is?"

"*Lo siento, Senorita*," the clerk said. "I am sorry, I do not."

"How about a livery stable?"

"Several blocks away," he said. "Just go out the front and turn left. You will not miss it."

She accepted her key, went to her room to drop off the saddlebags and rifle, then went back out to walk the horse to the livery.

Along the way she passed several galleries and realized they all featured paintings. The one she wanted would feature photographs. She wondered who would be able to direct her to it?

The livery she found was a small adobe building, with a young man lazing out front in a chair. When he saw her, he leaped to his feet and removed his hat.

"May I help you, Ma'am?"

"I just need to put my horse up for a few days," she said.

"You can do that here," he said. "I'll take very good care of your horse."

She decided not to go inside the building—not after recent events.

"Can you take him in for me and unsaddle him?"

"Of course," he said. "And I'll brush him down and feed him."

"How much will it cost me?"

"Not much," he said. "We're real small. You can settle up when you leave."

"Good," she said. "Thanks. I'm at a hotel just a few blocks from here."

"I know it," he said.

"How do you know which one I'm talking about?"

"My cousin runs it," he said. "He has the clerk send his guests here."

That was fine with her, as long as they cared for her animal.

"Oh," she said, before leaving, "I'm looking for a gallery."

"We have lots of those."

"But the one I'm looking for doesn't carry paintings," she said. "It's about photographs."

"Oh," he said, "there ain't so many of those."

"Can you tell me where the Mathew Brady Gallery is?" she asked.

"I never heard of it," he said, "but I can find out."

"I'd appreciate it," she said. "Just send word to the hotel."

"I'll do that," he said.

Hopefully, she would have found it by then herself, but if not . . .

"What's your name?" she asked.

"Jamie."

"I'm Roxy," she said. "Thanks, Jamie."

"My pleasure, Miss Roxy."

"Just Roxy," she said. "No Miss."

"Okay, Roxy!"

She turned and headed back toward her hotel.

***

Before reaching the hotel she came upon a gallery that had not only paintings in its window, but some blankets as well as clay pots and figurines. She stopped to look, and as the aromas wafted to her nostrils from the café next door her stomach began to rumble.

She followed her nose to the front door of the restaurant. She could hear conversations inside, knew it was approaching suppertime so there'd be plenty of people inside. She preferred to eat in cafes and restaurants during their off hours, when there weren't so many people at nearby tables to stare at her. This was not an exaggerated opinion of herself. She knew people stared at her for several different reasons.

However, she was just too hungry at that moment to wait. Also, if she was unable to get a table near the back, there was no large window in the front of the place, so it wasn't likely someone would spot her and decide to take a shot at her.

She stepped inside and let all the delicious smells surround her.

Chapter Eight

As expected she was stared at, but she felt it was mostly because she was a stranger. Getting a table in the back wasn't a problem, because no one else seemed to want those tables. Most of the diners were families of two, three or four, seated in the center of the room.

Roxy preferred waitresses to waiters. She got along with them and didn't have to fend off any clumsy advances during her meal.

"It smells great in here," she told the middle-aged woman who came to take her order.

The woman laughed. "That's usually what brings visitors in here, the smell. It's just a variety of spices the cook uses in his dishes."

"On steak?" Roxy asked.

"Oh, yeah," the woman said, "and on the vegetables."

"Then that's what I'll have."

"Comin' right up."

"Can I get a cold beer with it?"

"I'll bring it right out."

True to her word the waitress returned fairly quickly with a mug of cold beer, told Roxy her steak would be right out.

Roxy sipped the beer while she waited, enjoying the way the cold liquid cleared the trail dust from her throat. She looked around, studying the other occupants of the café. Again she noticed that no one was paying any special attention to her, which was fine. She had not been to New Mexico in her search for her father over the years, sticking to the Western regions of the country—Arizona, Nevada, even Colorado and Wyoming. These were the areas her father seemed to have made his reputation in. She knew now, however, that it was probably time for her to broaden her search. Not only New Mexico, but possibly Texas, Kansas, states closer to the Mississippi.

She didn't want to even think about how long it would take her to find him if he had hung up his guns, retired from hunting bounty and moved back East, where they had originally emigrated from.

Even though she was 15 when she left the Mormon community in Utah where her father had left her, she had only been searching for him in deadly earnest for the past 5 or 6 years. Before that she'd had to grow up, learn how to be a woman rather than a girl. And even then it had only been through her mentorship under Clint Adams, the Gunsmith, that she had truly come to terms with who she was.

She had a reputation, now, one that preceded her, and she often wondered if her father had heard of her. But if he had, why would he not contact her?

She had many, many questions for him when she finally did find him, and maybe this photo, this portrait from the Brady studio would finally lead her to him.

The waitress came out with a steaming plate with a huge steak and a mound of vegetables on it.

"There ya go, sweetie," she said, setting it down in front of her. "Enjoy, and if you want somethin' else—oh, damn. I forgot the biscuits. I'll be right back."

She hurried back to the kitchen, then returned with a basket of warm biscuits and some butter.

"There you go, that looks like everything," she said. "Just give me a holler if you want anythin' else—or if you just want more."

"Thank you."

As the waitress moved away Roxy cut into the steak and found it perfect, just red and tender enough. When she put the first chunk into her mouth she knew what the woman had meant about special spices. Whatever the cook had put on the steak, it was delicious.

She finished her meal and took the waitress' advice about having a piece of pie and some coffee.

"How was everythin'?" the woman asked, when she handed Roxy her check.

"Wonderful," Roxy said, paying her. "And maybe you can help me, while I'm here."

"Sure, hon. Whataya need?"

"I need to find a gallery."

"Got one right next store," the waitress said.

"The one I need to find deals in photographs, not paintings or pots."

"Ah," the waitress said, screwing up her face, "don't think I know any of those. Did you ask next door?"

"No, I didn't go in."

"You should," the waitress said. "Randolph is a wonderful artist, and he might be able to tell you where to find what you're lookin' for. He pretty much knows everybody around here."

"Randolph?"

"Henry Randolph," she said. "Tell him I sent you in. But watch out for him."

"How do you mean?"

"You're a beautiful girl, and he's a lady's man," the waitress said. "That's all I'm gonna say."

"Thanks for the information, and the food . . . and the warning," Roxy said.

Chapter Nine

Roxy left the café and went next door to the gallery with the pots and blankets and paintings in the front window. She hadn't noticed before, but in the lower right hand corner of the window it said Randolph Gallery.

She opened the door and entered. The interior was quiet and empty, filled with more of what was in the window. There were paintings on the wall, blankets hanging on racks and clay pots on shelves. While she was looking around a man came through a curtained doorway in the back and stopped short when he saw her.

He was about six feet tall, with long hair that came to his shoulders, black streaked with grey, and a matching grey beard and mustache. She guessed his age to be somewhere in his early 50's, despite the grey. He was wearing a white shirt, with dark pants and suspenders.

"May I help you?" he asked, after they had examined each other for several seconds.

"I was eating next door and the waitress suggested I come in here."

"That would be Sandra," the man said. "I'll have to thank her."

"You have some very interesting things here," Roxy said. "Are all of these your work?"

"Actually," Randolph said, "the paintings are mine. The blankets and pots come from other artists, who don't have galleries, show I show them here."

"And when you sell them?"

"I give them the money."

"That's very nice of you."

"Are you looking for something in particular?" he asked.

"Actually," she said, "what I'm looking for isn't here."

"That's a shame," he said. "What is it? Maybe I can . . . get it for you."

"I'm looking for a specific gallery, but nobody seems to know where it is."

"What's it called?"

"The Mathew Brady Gallery."

"Mathew Brady is a photographer," he said.

"Yes, I know," she said. "I'm looking for a photograph."

"An existing one, or do you want one taken?" he asked.

"An existing one," she said. "It's a portrait."

"Ah," he said, "well, I do know of the Brady Gallery. It's new in town and located off the beaten path."

"Can you tell me where it is?"

"I suppose I could tell you," he said, "and give you directions, but perhaps it would be better if I took you there myself."

"Oh, I wouldn't want to bother you while you're working," she protested.

"As you can tell," he said, "I'm not having a very busy day. I'll just lock the door and take you there. Perhaps we can get better acquainted along the way."

35

"Maybe we can," she agreed.

"I have a buggy out back," he said. "I need only to hitch the horse up."

"I can help."

"Then let me lock the front door," he said, "we'll go out the back."

She was thinking he might be trying to get her into his back room, but when they entered it he simply led the way across to the door in the rear wall. All around them were easels with paintings on them in various states of progress.

"You know," he said, "you are extraordinarily beautiful. I would love to paint you."

She saw one painting of a woman she thought she recognized, who had posed totally nude. And then she realized who it was.

"This is Sandra," she said, "the waitress, isn't it?"

"Yes, it is," he said. "She comes in and poses for me from time to time."

"And would you be wanting to paint me like . . . this?" she asked.

"We could discuss that," he said, "if you're willing to pose."

"What about with my gun?" she asked.

"We could do that," he said. Then he had a thought. "Do you mean . . . just with the gun?"

"We could discuss that."

***

Out back was a buggy and a horse in a leanto. Roxy waited while the artist hitched the horse to the buggy, and then he helped her up onto the seat.

"Is it very far away?" she asked.

He climbed aboard next to her and picked up the reigns. After hitching the horse up, he had donned a black jacket and hat.

"As I said," he replied, "it's a little off the beaten path. If it becomes successful I'm sure it will move to a more public location."

"Do you think it will be successful?" she asked.

"Why don't we wait until we get there," he suggested, "and then you can tell me."

Chapter Ten

"You haven't heard of Brady before?" he asked, as they rode.

"Not until I saw the newspaper," she said. "I guess he was very busy during the Civil war?"

"Oh yes," Randolph said, "he made a name for himself on the battlefields.

"Taking photos of bodies?" she asked.

"Yes, for being on the battlefields with a camera, rather than with a gun."

"Oh, I see. So he's a brave man?"

"I don't know him," Randolph said, "but I would guess he'd have to be, wouldn't you?"

"I suppose."

"If you don't know him, and didn't know of him, why are you looking for him?"

"There was a photo in the newspaper of someone I thought I recognized," she said. "I'm trying to find him."

"Well," Randolph said, "I hope they'll be able to help you when we get there. And then maybe afterward, we can go out and celebrate your success."

"Maybe," she said.

***

They rode for a while, and Roxy was starting to think that Henry Randolph was simply giving her a scenic look at Santa Fe. At one point she thought she saw the same building she had seen once before and felt that maybe he was driving in circles. But finally, he reined the horse in and stopped the buggy in front of a small, adobe building, standing almost by itself. The surrounding buildings didn't seem to be occupied.

"This is it?" she asked.

"This is it."

He got down from the buggy and then assisted her in getting down.

"Would you like me to come in with you?" he asked.

"Since you don't know anyone, I think I can manage introducing myself. Thanks for the ride."

"You want me to leave you here?" he asked.

"Well, I don't know exactly how long I'll be."

"That's all right," he said. "I closed my gallery and have nothing else to do. And you'll need a ride back to your hotel."

"I suppose I will."

"And we did talk about possibly celebrating together," he said. "That is, if you have success here."

"All right, then," she said. "I'll try not to be too long."

"Don't worry about me," he said, leaning against the buggy. "I'll roll myself a cigarette."

Roxy turned, went to the front door, which was solid wood. There were windows in the front of the building, but they were not displaying anything but dirt. There was not even a sign on the building's front announcing Mathew Brady Gallery. She tried the door and found it unlocked.

The inside looked much better than the outside. It was cleaner, with photographs displayed on easels set up around the room.

Nobody was there to talk to, but she heard noise coming from a back room, and walked to that open doorway.

"Hello?"

A man who had his head bent over something looked up at her with wide, liquid eyes behind wire-framed glasses. He was young, in his twenties, very tall and thin.

"Yes, hello. Uh, I'll be with you in a minute, if you'll just wait in the, uh, gallery?"

"Sure."

She backed away from the door and began to stroll around the room, looking at photos on the easels. She stopped short when she came to one in particular—the one that had drawn her attention in the newspaper.

The one she thought was her father, Gavin Doyle.

***

It took several minutes for the young man to finish what he was doing and come out of the back room. Wiping his hands on a dirty rag, he tossed it aside. He was also wearing a fairly grimy white apron that covered him from chest to ankles.

"I'm sorry," he said, "I was in the middle of something. Can I help you?"

"Yes, you can," she said, pointing. "This photograph. Who took it?"

He walked to join her in front of the easel and looked surprised.

"This one?" he asked. "You like this one. We have many others, some of them Civil War scenes—"

"No," she said, "just this one."

"Well, this *is* the Mathew Brady Gallery—"

"You're not Mathew Brady," she said.

"Um, well, no," he answered, "but I work with Mr. Brady."

"Work with him?"

"Yes, as an assistant," the young man said. "In fact, many of the photographs he has taken credit for have been shot by me, and by other assistants."

"Then how can he take credit?" she asked.

"Well, they're using his equipment, and his techniques–"

"So then who took this one?"

"This one?" he asked. "Well, I'd have to look that up—"

"Do it."

"See here, you can't be ordering me around—"

She put her hand on her gun. "This says I can, don't you think?"

"Uh, well, yes, I suppose—"

"Look it up."

"May I ask . . . why are you so interested in this particular portrait?"

"Because that man," she said, pointing, "might be my father."

"Oh!" He seemed very surprised. "Oh, my, really? I, uh—"

"What's your name?" she asked.

"It's Bill—uh, William Benson."

"Mr. Benson," she said, "why do I have the feeling that you don't have to look up the information on this photograph at all?"

"Um, well, yes, this *is* sort of a special case."

"Answer me this," she said, "before we go on. Is this a portrait of Gavin Doyle, the bounty hunter?"

"Um, well, yes," he said, "yes, it is."

Chapter Eleven

Roxy wanted to shout, "Yes!" but she didn't. It wasn't time, yet.

"Did you take this photograph?" she asked.

"Uh, well, no, I didn't."

"Then Mathew Brady did?"

"No."

"Okay, I don't understand," she said. "Do you work for Mathew Brady or not?"

"I did," Benson said, "but I don't, anymore."

"So you left, or he fired you."

"Yes."

"Which is it?"

"Well . . . fired."

"So this is not really a Mathew Brady gallery."

"Uhhhhhh, no," he drawled.

"Where is the Mathew Brady Gallery?"

Benson screwed up his face. "There isn't really one."

"Was there ever a man named Mathew Brady?"

"Oh yes," Benson said, "he was very popular during the Civil War. People enjoyed seeing depictions of the battles. It showed them what their loved ones were going through. The photographs appeared in all sorts of private collections."

"But?"

"But after the war was over, it changed," Benson said. "People didn't want to dwell on those events, didn't want to look at them, anymore. Suddenly, Mathew couldn't sell his photographs. He had to close his studio. And then his eyesight started to go. When photographs were taken, they were taken by assistants."

"And?"

"In eighteen seventy-five Congress gave him twenty-five thousand dollars, because he had spent so much money during the war. But right now, Mathew is almost penniless."

"Where is he?"

"In New York."

"Why did you decide to open a fake gallery here, in Santa Fe."

"Well, I wanted to be as far from Mathew as I could," Benson said. "And I was hoping to trade on his name out here until I could establish myself."

"So have any of these photographs actually been taken by you?"

"Not yet," he said. "I haven't started."

"But you do have Brady photographs here."

"Yes . . . some."

"Enough to call it a Mathew Brady Gallery."

"Yes."

"And you stole them?"

"Well, stole—"

"You stole them!"

"Yes," he said, "y-yes, I stole them."

"Okay, then where did you steal this one from? Did Brady take it?"

"No, this is not a Brady."

"And it's not a Benson."

He looked pained. "No."

"Then what is it? Who took it?"

"Well, it's . . . it's a Fly."

"A Fly?" she repeated. "Who's Fly?"

"Buck Fly is a photographer who has a gallery in Tombstone."

"And he takes portrait photographs like this one?"

"Actually, he considers himself more of a photojournalist. He travels and takes photographs, then sells them to newspapers."

"And when did he take this photograph?"

"That I don't know."

"But you know he took it in Tombstone?"

"He don't know that, either."

"Well, what do you know?"

"I know that Fly has a boarding house and gallery in Tombstone. He runs it with his wife, Mollie."

"And how do you know this?"

"I ran into Fly in Arizona, down near the Mexican border. He was selling photographs."

"And he sold you this one?"

"Yes," Benson said, "cheap."

"So this one you didn't steal."

"No."

"Why did you want it?"

Benson shrugged. "I liked it."

"And he told you it was a photograph of Gavin Doyle?" she asked.

"Yes, he did."

"If you're lying to me—"

"I'm not, I'm not!" he insisted.

She looked at the portrait again. This close up, and this large—it threatened to fall off the easel—she could see her father in the face—the eyes mostly. He was staring sternly ahead of him, probably right at the photographer, Buck Fly.

"I want this," she said.

"Take it!"

"I can't," she said. "I can't travel around with it, and I have no place to put it." She turned to look at him. "Do you know who I am?"

"N-no," he said. "Only that you say you're Gavin Doyle's daughter."

"That's right," she said. "I'm Roxy Doyle."

"Who? Wait. Who?" He suddenly got it. "Roxy—you mean, Lady Gunsmith?"

"That's right."

"Lady Gunsmith is Gavin Doyle's daughter?"

"Right, again."

"Jesus . . . well, s-sure, you can have it."

"I need you to keep it for me," she said. "Take it off display, don't let anybody see it, and hold it until I come back for it."

"Well . . . I can do that."

"When I come back, if it's not here I'll make you pay."

He swallowed.

"And if you're not here, I'll make you pay."

"S-so, you're not gonna close me down?"

46

"No," she said. "You can run this gallery as long as you want—but you better be here, with this portrait, when I get back."

"When will that be?" he asked.

"I don't know," she said, "but whenever it is, you better be here."

"Yes, Ma'am," he said. "I-I'll be here."

She looked at the photograph again.

"If I go to Tombstone to see this Fly fella," she said, "and he tells me something different from what you told me, you'll regret it."

"No, no," he said, "don't worry, he'll tell you just what I told you . . . and more!"

"He better," she said.

"But like I said, he travels, some," Benson said, "but his wife, Mollie, she'll be there."

"Mollie Fly?"

He nodded.

She shook her head. The poor woman.

"Take this off the easel and put it in your back room," she said.

"Yes, Ma'am, right away."

"Well, do it! I want to watch."

Hurriedly, he fetched a cloth large enough to cover the photograph, then lifted it from the easel and took it to the back room.

"I'm leaving," she said, when he returned. "Remember everything I said. Don't make me have to come looking for you."

"No, Ma'am," he said. "You won't."

"I better not."

She turned and left the gallery.

Chapter Twelve

Randolph was leaning against the buggy, smoking a cigarette, when she came out.

"Did you find what you were looking for?" he asked.

"I did."

"Where is it?"

"He's holding it for me until I find someplace to put it," she said.

"I can take it to my gallery," he said. "And hold it for you."

"I might take you up on that," she said. "I'll have to let you know."

"So where to now?"

"I'd like to go back to my hotel."

"What about later?" he asked. "A celebratory supper?"

She hesitated.

"I know a very nice restaurant," he said. "Good steaks, and wine. A great place to celebrate. And talk about whether or not you'll pose for me."

"All right," she said. "Take me to my hotel, and we'll have supper later."

"Excellent!" he said, happily.

***

In her room Roxy sat on the bed with her hands clutching her thighs, tears of frustration streaming down her face. Then she impatiently wiped them away with the heels of her hands. Nothing was definite yet, except that she was going to leave Santa Fe in the morning and head for Tombstone, Arizona. It would take her at least a week to get there, unless she pushed her new steel dust and rode him into the ground. But what was the difference, one day more or less? Fly's Gallery, or whatever it was, would still be there.

Probably the best thing for her to do right now was get ready to have supper with the artist, Henry Randolph—and maybe a little more. Just to relax her, of course.

***

She had washed as well as she was able to use the pitcher-and-basin in her room, changed her clothes, and went down to wait for Randolph in front of the hotel. While sitting there, though, another man approached her—tall, sturdy and alone, wearing a badge.

"'Good-evenin'," he greeted.

"'evenin', Sheriff."

"You mind if we have a talk?"

"Would it matter if I did?" she asked. "After all, you're the law."

He grabbed another chair, dragged it over and sat down next to her.

"I'm Sheriff Cole Wagner," he said.

"Okay."

"And you're Roxy Doyle?"

"That's right."

"Mind if I ask what brings you to town?"

"A love of art."

"Ah," Wagner said, "our galleries."

"Yes."

"How many have you seen, so far?"

"Just two."

"How much longer will you be in town?"

"I'm leaving tomorrow morning."

"After seein' only two galleries?"

"I've seen enough."

"So there'll be no trouble?"

"Not unless somebody causes it tomorrow before I can ride out of town."

"And what about tonight?"

"I'm just going to have a meal," she said.

"Where?"

"I don't know, yet."

"Want a recommendation?"

"No."

"Just thought I'd offer."

He stood up.

"You mind if I ask who told you I was here?"

"You're a noticeable woman, Miss Doyle," he said. "Nobody had to tell me."

She wondered if the young man, Benson, had gone to the sheriff after she talked with him.

"You sure somebody didn't complain?"

"About what?" he asked. "You said you were only here to look at galleries. What's there to complain about?"

"Nothing," she said.

"Exactly." He touched the brim of his hat. "Have a nice supper."

"Thanks."

He crossed over to the other side of the street and headed left. She watched until he was out of sight. Then, from the right, Henry Randolph appeared.

"Ah, how very punctual," he said. "Or am I late?" He was wearing a black suit, a string tie and a black hat with a silver band. She felt underdressed.

"I just thought I'd sit out here and wait," she said. "And I had a visitor."

"Oh? Who?"

"The sheriff."

"Sheriff Wagner?" He looked puzzled at that. "What did he want?"

"What they all want when I come to town," she said. "For there to be no trouble."

"And what did you tell him?"

"That I'd be leaving in the morning."

He frowned.

"Is that true?"

"Yes."

"I can't convince you to stay and model for me, first?" he asked.

"No."

"May I try, over supper?"

"Oh, yes, you can try," she said, "as long as the meal is good."

"I'll take you to the best restaurant in town," he said. "All kinds of delicacies for you to choose from."

"Good," she said. "I'm suddenly very hungry."

Chapter Thirteen

He kept his promise and took her to an excellent restaurant. It was very large, taking up almost half a block. Nearby was the Santa Fe plaza where many shops had items for sale. There were also Indians sitting on blankets outside the shops, selling hand-crafted pots and jewelry.

The place was called The Hacienda Steakhouse, but Randolph had promised her that it did more than just steaks.

"You'll have plenty to choose from."

Once again he drove them there in his buggy, and left it right outside the door, with the horse tied to a post.

"Ah, Mr. Randolph," a man greeted as soon as they entered. "Welcome back."

"Thanks, Charles. I brought a friend with me and promised her a memorable meal."

The man, also wearing a black suit, bowed to Roxy and said, "We will try to satisfy the lovely lady."

"Thank you," she said.

"You're usual table, sir?"

Randolph looked at Roxy.

"It's in front, by the window," he told her.

"May we try another one," she said, and then to Charles, "one in the back?"

"Of course. This way, please."

When they were seated Randolph smiled and asked, "Is it that you don't want to be seen with me?"

"I don't want to be seen from the outside, period," she said. "It would be too easy for somebody to take a shot at me."

"Oh, yes," he said, "now I feel like a fool. Of course, you have to consider such things."

"No problem," she said. "That's something you should never have to think about."

A waiter came to the table and gave them each a printed menu.

"So many choices," she said, "as promised."

"If you like," Randolph said, "I could order for both of us."

"Sure," she said, "why not?"

He took the menu from her and handed it back to the waiter.

He ordered them each a bowl of tortilla soup, followed by something called beef Wellington. He also asked the waiter to bring a bottle of red wine.

As the waiter walked away he said, "It's steak, but prepared unlike any you've ever had."

"I look forward to it," she said.

"And I'll order dessert after."

The waiter brought the wine, poured two glasses, and left the bottle.

She tasted it, didn't like it, but tried to keep the distaste off her face.

"How is it?" he asked.

"It's fine," she said. "I'm, not usually a wine drinker."

"I could get something else," he offered.

"No, no," she said, "this will do."

"It'll taste better with the food."

She doubted it but smiled at the comment.

"Now," he said, "back to the business at hand."

"Business?"

"The business of you posing," he said. "Did you think I would ask you to pose for free?"

"You want to pay me to pose?"

"Yes," he said. "I often pay my models, although some of them are quite happy to do it for nothing."

"Mr. Randolph—"

"Henry, please."

"Henry," she said, "if I was going to sit for you, I'd do it for free. I just don't have the time."

"And if you did have the time," he asked, "would I be able to convince you to pose . . . nude?"

"That I don't know about," she said. "I usually prefer to be nude in private."

"Well, there would be no one there but the two of us," he assured her. "That part of my gallery is always closed to the public. I don't let anyone see me when I work."

"I understand," she said. "Maybe, if I'm back this way again—"

"Is it very important for you to leave tomorrow?" he asked.

"I'm afraid it is," she said.

"How about this?" he asked, pouring her some more wine. "You come to my gallery tonight and I will sketch you. Then I can work on the painting after you leave."

"You can paint me from a sketch?" she asked.

"Oh yes," he said, "I often work from sketches. Of course, I prefer to work with live models, but this would be a special case. Really, I can't let a woman as beautiful as you get away. What kind of an artist would I be?"

The waiter came with their soup.

"We can talk about it some more over the meal," Randolph said to her.

"All right," she agreed, nodding. "We can at least talk about it."

***

The beef Wellington was so good Roxy didn't want to talk while she ate it. Randolph understood, but he watched her the entire time, until she'd had enough.

"Why do you keep doing that?" she asked.

"What?"

"Watching me eat."

"I'm sorry," he said. "I'm not really watching, I'm just studying you with an artist's eye."

"And what do you see?"

"Well," he said, "I see somebody who should be painted. Or, at least, sketched."

"Look—"

"How about this?" he asked. "You really didn't see much of my shop when you came by. Come back there with me and have a look at what I do, and how I do it. Then whatever you decide, I'll abide by. I won't bother you, anymore."

She thought a moment.

"All right," she said. "I feel like I owe you for this meal, so we'll do that."

"You don't owe me for this at all," he said, "but if that's what it takes to get you to come by, it's okay with me."

Chapter Fourteen

Henry Randolph unlocked the front door of his gallery and allowed Roxy to precede him. She already knew she was going to have sex with him, and that he would probably be the oldest man she had ever been with. It should be interesting.

But she wasn't going to give in to him that easily. She intended to make him work for it. Then, when they did have sex, it would relax her enough for her to sleep soundly that night and be ready to leave early the next morning for Tombstone.

But first the gallery, and the games.

"Let's go in the back," he said. "I'll show you some of my work."

"All right."

They went into the rear and he lit two lamps, which flooded the room with light. The first painting he showed her was one she had seen earlier, of the waitress next door, Sandra.

"How hard was it for you to get her to take her clothes off?" Roxy asked.

"Not hard," he said. "First we had sex. After that her clothes were already off, so it didn't take much convincing."

He walked over to one wall, brought back two more paintings, also nudes of different women, with dark hair, and the other a blonde.

"They were all smiling," he told her. "It's not that I painted a smile on their faces."

"Smiling," she said, "because you had sex with them before you painted them?"

"Of course."

"Do you sleep with all your models?"

"But I have to," he said. "It's the only way I can capture the essence of my subject."

"So your models are always young women?" she asked.

"You think I take advantage?" he asked. "Wait, look." He went and got another painting, one that had been facing the wall. When he turned it, she saw a naked woman, also smiling at the painter, but not young.

"This is Edna," he said, "she was sixty-five when I painted this."

The woman had sagging breasts, loose skin around her neck and belly, and yet there was something lovely about her.

"And you slept with her?"

"Yes," he said, "we made love several times, and then she sat for me."

"Do you ever paint men?"

Randolph blew air out of his mouth and said, "Oh, no! Only women. You're all so lovely, I just have to find that beauty and bring it out."

"Well," Roxy said, "you did it for Edna. She looks . . . happy."

"She was," he said, "but I don't know if she was happier with the sex, or the painting."

"Which were you happier with?"

"Oh," he said, "the painting, of course. I am an artist first, and then a man."

"So which one wants me to take off my clothes?"

"Ah, well you, that's a special case," Randolph said. "I've painted many women, but I've never seen one as beautiful as you. Can you imagine what I can do for you in a painting, starting with the beauty you already possess?"

"But we'd have to have sex first."

"Well, yes," he said. "Is that a problem. Am I so . . . unappealing?"

"No."

"Too old, then?" he asked. "I am only fifty-two. How old are you?"

"Half that."

"Ah!" he said, as if he now understood her reluctance.

"It's not your age," she said. "You're a very attractive man."

"What, then?"

She looked at the paintings again. A man who could make these women look so beautiful. Sandra, the waitress, who looked faded and close to middle age, after sleeping with Randolph and being painted by him, looked beautiful. And Edna, 65 years old but looking so happy and lovely . . . and the other women . . .

"When I sleep with a man," she said, "I generally want it to be forgotten the next day. I can't afford to fall in love, or have a man fall in love with me. I'll be moving on tomorrow . . ."

"What if I promise not to fall in love with you?" he asked.

She laughed.

"But what if I fall in love with you?"

"You won't."

"Why not?"

"I'm not worth falling in love with," he said. "I live only for my art. And yes, I'm too old for you. So if we sleep together tonight, and then I sketch you, I'll be able to paint after you leave. And some day, if you come back, I'll show your portrait to you."

"Promise?"

"I promise."

"All right, then," she said. "How do we start?"

"With a kiss?" he asked, coming closer.

Chapter Fifteen

The kiss was tentative at first, as they felt each other out, and then more insistent. Because of his age she was expecting to learn some things. She hoped she wouldn't be disappointed.

The way he kissed was no disappointment. It wasn't too rough, mashing her lips against her teeth like some men, and it wasn't too fleeting. The pressure of his lips on hers was just right.

She was also impressed by his hands. They did not grab and prod her insistently, or squeeze. He stroked her, lightly brushing the back of his hand over her breasts so that she felt it in her nipples. He was very knowing and experienced, which had been what she was hoping for. In her mind, this was not a night for a quick poke.

"Where—" she started to say, but he stopped her.

"Come with me."

He took her hand, walked her to another doorway she hadn't seen before, since it was behind some screens. Inside was a small room with a bed that almost filled it.

"You have a bed here," she said. "Very sneaky."

"Not sneaky," he said. "There's no point in doing this on the floor, or against the wall. I want my model to feel cared for, and respected."

"There are so many men who know nothing about what you're saying," she commented.

"The problem with young men," he said, "is that they're young." He raised both his hands to her throat level. "May I?"

It took her a moment to see what he was asking.

"Oh yes," she said, "please do."

Slowly, he began to unbutton her shirt. When he had it open he reached inside, stroked her skin, kissed her again, and then slid the shirt off her gently, letting it aside.

He removed the rest of her clothing with the same care— except for her gunbelt. She did that, and set it aside, where it would be within easy reach.

When she was completely naked she slid up onto the bed, sat with her back against the pillow which she propped against the wall, and watched him disrobe.

He undressed slowly, and rather than toss his clothes aside he folded them before laying them down. When he was completely naked he stood there a moment, so she could have a look. His penis was not fully hard yet, but impressive, jutting from his pubic bush. She wondered if he'd been even bigger as a young man, but perhaps, at 52, he was as vital as ever.

He had swirls of dark hair on his chest, which she liked. As he crawled onto the mattress with her, she reached out and tangled her fingers in it. Then, when he was close enough, she slid one hand down into his pubic hair, gripped it, then slid the hand up the length of his cock, feeling the heat and smoothness of it against her palm.

When he put his hands on her breasts she caught her breath. Those artists' hands seemed so different from any others she had experienced. He cupped her breasts, feeling their weight, and then stroked them until her nipples were aching.

Then he leaned forward and kissed first the upper slopes, then the full undersides, and finally the nipples themselves. He gave every part to her breasts equal attention. Young men always seemed to focus on her nipples, chewing on them like a cow on its cud. This man knew what he was doing every second. But of course he did. When he painted his women, he wanted them to be glowing with satisfaction. Suddenly she knew that was what he was able to capture in his paintings, an inner happiness. It turned a faded waitress into a beautiful woman. What would it do for her?

Suddenly she was upset she couldn't sit for him and see the painting when it was finished. She hoped he'd be able to capture her while working from a sketch.

But at the moment he was capturing her in every other way possible. She slid down so that she was no longer leaning against the wall but was on her back. He kissed down her body, his lips flitting across her skin, leaving a tingling trail behind. And when his face was nestled in her tangle of hair down there, his tongue darted through and found her wet and wanting.

Most men didn't do this, and the ones who did licked and sucked and gobbled like pigs in a sty. The only other man she'd ever been with who made her feel this way was Clint Adams. Both Clint and Randolph seemed to know what a woman wanted, and they knew how to give it to her.

When she felt the trembling beginning in her thighs and her belly she reached down for his head and grasped it.

"Don't stop," she whispered, "don't stop . . ."

But he had no intention of stopping. He took her right over the edge with his mouth and tongue, and stayed with her, tasting it all, not letting any of her passionate essence go to waste . . .

***

Later he mounted her, entered her, and she was transported again by the feel of his penis inside of her. This time, instead of examining it, or wondering about it, she gave herself up to it. He grabbed her legs, spread them even wider, and took her in long, hard strokes, his muscles standing out as he came close to his release, and then there it was, exploding inside of her like thousands of hot needles . . .

Chapter Sixteen

Later, he posed her in the back room, among the easels, and stood behind one in particular, sketching what he saw. They were both still naked.

"I don't have to bring your beauty out," he told her, "I just hope I can capture it on the canvas."

"From what I've seen, you're talented enough to do anything," she said.

He kept flipping pages, as he did sketch after sketch, trying to get it right.

Finally he asked, "How about the guns."

The gun and holster were right next to the stool she was seated on. She looked down at them.

"You want me to hold the gun?"

"No," he said, "how about wearing it."

"While I'm naked?"

"Yes."

She shrugged, stood up, picked up the holster and strapped it around her naked waist. She had not expected to be able to pose for him nude, but after the sex it suddenly seemed the right and easy thing to do.

But now, standing there wearing her gun and nothing else, she felt . . . silly? Embarrassed? She wasn't even sure.

"Are you sure about this?" she asked.

"Just let me sketch you," he said, "and I'll decide later which pose to use for the portrait."

"Standing or sitting?"

"Stand, please," he said. "Look at me like you're about to draw the gun."

She did as he asked, feeling the dirt floor of the room beneath her bare feet. It was also warm back there. They'd been sweating during sex, cooled off, and now she was starting to heat up, again.

"It's getting late," she told him. "I have to get an early start in the morning."

"I'm done, I'm done," he said, setting the sketch pad aside.

"Can I see—"

"No, no," he said, "they're just sketches. I don't show those to anyone. You'll have to come back to see the painting."

She unstrapped the gun and started to get dressed.

"You can spend the night here," he said, "or come home with me. I have a small house and a big bed."

"If I spend the night with you," she said, "I probably won't be in any condition to ride tomorrow."

"That's what I was hoping for."

Fully dressed, she strapped the gunbelt back on.

"I have to go, Henry."

"I know," he said. "Thank you for posing."

She walked to him and kissed him on the cheek.

"Make me beautiful," she said.

"I don't have any choice," he assured her. "You are beautiful."

He walked to the door with her while he was still naked and stood in the doorway as she took his buggy.

"Just leave it at your hotel and I'll pick it up later," he said.

"Thank you, Henry, for everything. Your help, the painting . . . everything."

"Believe me, Roxy," he said, "it was all my pleasure. I hope you find what you're looking for."

"Wait!" she said, as he started to shut the door.

"Change your mind?" he asked, hopefully.

"About one thing," she said. "I don't trust that fellow Benson at the Brady Gallery. Will you go and pick up that photograph for me and hold it here?"

"Of course," he said. "At least that way I know you'll come back, eventually."

"That's true," she assured him.

***

She drove the buggy to her hotel, left it out front as Henry had requested. She just hoped that nobody would steal it before morning.

When she went inside the desk clerk perked up, smiled and waited, hoping she was going to come to the desk.

She did.

"There's a horse and buggy out front," she said. "It belongs to a man named Henry Randolph. He'll be by to pick it up in the morning." She leaned on the desk. "I want it to still be there when he comes."

"Of course, Miss Doyle," the clerk said, "whatever you say."

"I say it better be there."

"Oh, it will."

"And I'm checking out in the morning."

"So soon? Don't you like our town?"

"I like it fine," she said. "I just have someplace to be."

"Yes, Ma'am. Good-night, Ma'am."

"Good-night," she told him, "and when I come down in the morning to pay my bill, don't call me 'Ma'am.'"

PART TWO

POWDERKEG

Chapter Seventeen

Tombstone, Arizona
August 1881

When Roxy Doyle rode down the main street of Tombstone—which was called Allen Street, unlike most towns who named their main street Main Street—she had no idea of the potential hornet's nest she was riding into.

Since she still had a good portion of the money she had won in the sharpshooting contest in Blackhawk, Colorado she decided not to spend too much time looking for a hotel. Instead, she simply rode up to the Grand Hotel and dismounted.

She knew she had attracted attention riding down the street—she actually saw two men with badges watching her from opposite sides—but she couldn't be concerned with that. She had to get the mundane things done first: paying for a room and getting the horses settled in a livery. After that she'd go looking for Fly's Gallery.

***

Sheriff Johnny Behan hated the Earps.

Ever since they came to Tombstone they had been trying to run roughshod over everybody, especially him and the Clantons. So at some point, Behan and the Clantons were going to take care of the Earps.

But at the moment he was more concerned with the ride coming down Allen Street. She wore a gun and had red hair. Now she could have been just anybody, but since Tombstone tended to attract trouble, Behan assumed he was right in thinking that this was Roxy Doyle, the Lady Gunsmith.

More trouble had just come to town.

***

After being appointed temporary Town Marshal several times for several reasons, Virgil Earp was finally named permanent marshal in June. His deputy was his brother, Morgan, and if he needed more deputies both his brother Wyatt and their friend, Doc Holiday would be available.

Virgil knew things were going to come to a head with the cowboys in town, led by Ike Clanton and Curly Bill Brocious. Also, things had been brewing between Johnny Ringo and Doc Holiday. But on this day, while he was walking the streets making his rounds, seeing the rider who was coming down the street, he knew that a new dynamic had been added to the powderkeg that had become Tombstone's center.

A red haired fuse had just ridden into town.

***

"Yes, Ma'am," the desk clerk at the hotel said, "we have rooms."

"Then I'll have one," she said.

"Sign in, please." He turned the register book around for her. "You might be interested in knowing we have some famous people stayin' here."

"Is that right."

"Yep," the man said, proudly, "Wyatt Earp and Doc Holiday have rooms here. And for a while we even had Bat Masterson, until he left town."

"That's interesting," she said, turning the book back to him. "Can I have my key?"

"Sure thing Miss . . ." He squinted at the book ". . . Doyle?"

"That's right," she said. "Does that name mean anything to you?"

"Oh, no, Ma'am," he said, "not a thing. Here you go, Room 5, top of the stairs."

"As long as it doesn't overlook the street."

"Oh, it doesn't."

"Thanks."

As she went up the stairs to the second floor the clerk looked again at the name she'd written in the book, to make sure he'd seen it right.

He had.

***

In her room Roxy thought about Wyatt Earp and Doc Holliday being in not only the same town as she was, but the same building. She knew that Clint Adams was friends with Wyatt Earp, as well as Bat Masterson. He had talked to her about them while mentoring her. Not so much about Doc Holliday, but he knew him, too.

But she didn't need to meet these people. She only needed to get to Fly's Studio and find out about her father. But first she'd have to see to her horse. She was still riding the steel dust, and he was still in good shape, so she wanted to take care of him.

She left her room quickly and, just at that moment, a man was passing her door. She ran into him, knocking him off balance, because he was slightly built.

"Hey, take it easy," the man said.

"Oh, I'm so sorry," Roxy said. The man held a handkerchief over his mouth and coughed into it. "Are you all right?"

"Oh yes, I'm fine," he said, in a slight southern drawl. "In spite of how I look, I'm not that delicate. Are you all right?"

"I'm fine," she said. "I'm just in a hurry."

He wore a black hat and suit, and a holstered pistol on his hip. Also a white shirt beneath a floral patterned vest.

"Well, don't let me get in your way, Ma'am," he said. "I'll letcha go." He executed a slight bow.

"Thank you, and again, I'm so sorry."

She hurried off down the hall.

John "Doc" Holliday looked after her and said, softly, "My, my."

Chapter Eighteen

When Roxy got down to Allen Street she was determined to search every street in Tombstone until she found the Fly Photography Studio. But it was not on Allen Street or, apparently, on any of the main streets in town.

By mid-afternoon she was hungry. She had passed many of Tombstone's eateries, but one had stuck in her mind. She walked back to 5th and Allen Street and entered the Crystal Palace Saloon and Steakhouse. She ignored the saloon part for now and was shown to an isolated table by a bow-tied waiter.

"Would you like to see a menu, Ma'am?" asked the eager to please waiter.

"No," she said. "It says steakhouse outside. I'll have a steak and a cold beer."

"Comin' up, Ma'am." She didn't like being called "Ma'am" by a man who was obviously in his 40's, but let it go for now.

She looked around, saw that she had chosen a slow time to come in and eat, which suited her. She knew her appearance usually attracted attention, and it would be even more so here since she was a stranger in Tombstone.

Still, the men in the place kept an appreciative eye on her, and the women cast their disapproving glances her way. In other words, all was normal.

The waiter brought her the mug of cold beer first, and then the steaming plate of steak and vegetables. She usually preferred chicken, but she was in a steakhouse, after all.

"Can I get you anything else?" the waiter asked.

"Yes," she said, "may I have some more grilled onions?"

"Of course," he said. "I'll be right back."

She started eating, and when he brought the extra onions in a bowl she dumped them on top of everything—the steak, the potatoes, the carrots.

"Enjoy your meal, Ma'am," the waiter said.

"Thanks."

She went back to cutting into her steak, which was cooked perfectly.

***

"Who did you say rode in?" Ike Clanton asked Johnny Behan.

"A redhead," Behan said. "Wearin' a gun."

"A woman, you mean?" Clanton stuffed a tortilla into his mouth. They were sitting in a small cantina, eating Mexican food and drinking tequila.

"That's what I mean."

Clanton sat back.

"A redhaired woman with a gun," he said. "You ain't talkin' about Lady Gunsmith, are ya?"

"That's what I'm thinkin'," Behan said.

"So whataya gonna do, John?"

"Go and talk to 'er," Behan said. "See what she's doin' in Tombstone."

"That's a good idea," Clanton said. "Get 'er on our side. In fact, why don't you have Ringo do it?"

"Ringo ain't exactly a charmer when it comes to women, Ike," Behan said. "I'll do it, myself."

"Sure, that's right," Clanton said. "You're the one who's a charmer. Like with that actress in town."

"Never mind that," Behan said. "Just keep your boys in line while I talk to her. If they see 'er there's no tellin' what they'll do."

"My boys'll be just fine," Clanton said. "You just go and do yer job."

Behan nodded, and left the cantina.

***

"Who do you think she is?" Morgan Earp asked his brother, Virgil.

Virgil was sitting at his desk in the marshal's office, going through wanted posters.

"I know who I think she is," Virgil said. "I'm just checkin' these fliers before I talk to her."

"About what?" Morgan asked.

Virgil looked up at his brother.

"This place is already a powderkeg, with the Clantons and Ringo and all. We don't need anybody lightin' the fuse."

"You know who I think she is," Morgan said.

"Yeah, same as I do," Virgil said. "Roxy Doyle."

"Lady Gunsmith," Morgan said. "Clint Adams' protégé."

"Exactly." Virgil said, putting the stack of posters aside. "I guess I'll go and talk to her, see what she wants here."

"What about Johnny Behan?"

"What about him?"

"Well, he's the sheriff," Morgan said. "And he likes a pretty lady. You don't think he's gonna talk to 'er?"

"Maybe get 'er on his side, you mean?" Virgil asked. "The side of the Clantons and the cowboys?"

"Well, they've got Ringo," Morgan said, "and we got Doc. We're kinda even."

"You forget we got Wyatt," Virgil said.

Morgan smiled. "You think Wyatt would let us forget we got Wyatt?"

"I'll just go and talk to 'er," Virgil said.

"You want me to come along, protect you?" Morgan asked, with another grin.

"I think I can handle a lady by myself, Morg," Virgil said.

"Try tellin' that to your wife."

"My wife, your wife, what's the difference," Virgil asked, "they both got us by the balls."

Chapter Nineteen

Virgil knew the redhaired woman he thought was Roxy Doyle was in the Crystal Palace, so he started over there. Along the way, he saw Johnny Behan, coming from the opposite direction. They met right across the street from the Palace.

"Where you goin', Sheriff?" Virgil asked.

"What's it to you, Earp?" Behan asked.

"I think we might be goin' to the same place," Virgil told him.

Behan smiled. "Across the street, you mean?"

"That's right."

"For a steak?"

"Not exactly."

"Me, neither," Behan said. "Whataya know about that?"

"Look, Sheriff," Virgil said, "I know you're better at talkin' to women than I am, so why don't you let me go in first? Take my shot."

"You think we're both after the same thing?" Behan asked.

Virgil nodded. "Like makin' sure her gun ain't used against us."

"You think you can get her to side with you?" Behan asked. "The badge isn't going to help you, you know. We've both got one."

Behan was better educated than the Earps, dressed better, handled women better . . . but he wasn't on the right side.

"Yeah, I think I can," Virgil said.

"I tell you what, Virgil," Behan said. "Why don't we flip a coin?"

Virgil thought Behan must've been feeling his oats, because if there was one thing he didn't do better than the Earps, it was gamble.

"You're on," Virgil said.

***

Roxy saw the tall, slender man in the black suit enter the restaurant, look around and settle his eyes on her. She also saw the badge prominently displayed on his chest. He walked over to her table and stopped, the eyes of the other diners following him.

"Roxy Doyle?" he asked.

"Good guess," she said, "or did you go to my hotel?"

"I saw you ride in," he said. "But you're right, it was a guess. Do you mind if I sit?"

"That depends," she said. "Do you intend to introduce yourself, Marshal?"

"Virgil Earp," he said.

"Earp?"

"That's right."

"I hadn't heard that any of the Earps were here in Tombstone," she said. "But then, I've been on the move."

"Have been for a while," he said. "Morg, Jim, and Wyatt."

"Well, well the whole family," she said. "Well, pull up a chair, Marshal."

81

J.R. Roberts

Virgil pulled out the chair across from her, removed his hat and sat. He had an angular face, made more so by the mustache he sported.

"Can I offer you anything?" she asked. "Beer? Coffee? I was about to have dessert."

"Coffee would be fine."

She waved, and a waiter magically appeared at her table.

"Coffee for me and the Marshal, please," she said, "and a slice of apple."

"Comin' up, Ma'am."

"You get good service," he commented.

"I'm a good tipper," she said.

"As I told you," Virgil said, "I saw you ride in this morning."

"You did tell me that."

"Sheriff John Behan also saw you. He'll be in here to talk to you after we're through."

"And what have I done to deserve all this attention?" she asked. "Just ride in, get a hotel, and take a stroll around town?"

"Yes, I know," he said. "But we're sittin' on a bit of a powderkeg in Tombstone. Sheriff Behan and the Earps are on opposite sides."

"Ah, and both sides are going to try to recruit me, is that it?"

"I think Behan will try that," Virgil said. "And while I might invoke the name of our mutual friend, Clint Adams, I'm not gonna try to recruit you. I'll just say it would be good if you stayed on the sidelines and didn't join either side."

"I see."

The waiter returned with their coffee, and her pie.

"Anything else, Ma'am?"

"No, I'm good."

"Marshal?"

"'Nothin'.'"

The waiter withdrew.

"As I understand it," she said, "it's Wyatt who's good friends with Clint."

"That's true," Virgil said. "He also has another good friend in town, Doc Holliday. Clint was here for a while, but he left."

"He moves around as much as I do," Roxy observed.

"I know that," Virgil, said, sipping his coffee. "Look, Miss Doyle—"

"Roxy," she said, "since we're all friends with Clint."

"All right, Roxy," he said. "I'd just like to know what brings you to Tombstone?"

She sat back and chewed a hunk of apple pie.

"There's no reason why I shouldn't tell you," she said. "I'm looking for Fly's Photography Gallery."

"Fly's? Now what would you want with Camillus Sydney Fly? Folks around here just call him Buck."

"He's supposed to have taken a picture of my father," she said. "I want to talk to him about it."

"Your father?"

"Gavin Doyle."

He raised his eyebrows.

"The bounty hunter?" he asked.

"That's right."

"I thought he was . . ." Virgil started, but trailed off when he realized how tactless it would be.

"Dead?" she finished. "That's what some folks keep telling me, but I've been searching for him for years. I don't think he's dead."

"Well," Virgil said, "I can tell you where Fly's is."

"That would be helpful," she said, "because I walked all over town today and didn't see it."

"It's not on a main street," he said. "In fact, he backs up to the O.K. Corral. It's over on Fremont Street. Fact of the matter is, his wife Mollie runs a boarding house there, and Fly's studio is in the back."

"Fremont Street."

"That's right," Virgil said. "Three-twelve."

"I'm much obliged, Marshal."

"I expect you'll be wanting to pay your respects to brother Wyatt, seeing as how you're both such good friends with Clint Adams."

"That might not be a bad idea."

"Well, you can usually find him in the evenings, dealing Faro over at the Birdcage."

"You've been real helpful, Marshal."

"Somethin' you oughtta know, though."

"What's that?"

"Fly ain't here."

"Where is he?"

"Down around Mexico, taking pictures. Should be back pretty soon, though. Mollie's here. She can probably tell you more."

"Then I guess I'll go and talk to Mollie," Roxy said. "I'll finish my pie and coffee first."

"And I might as well give John Behan his chance to talk with you," Virgil said, standing.

"Is he waiting outside?"

"That he is."

"Well, how did you fellas decide who was going to come in first?"

"We flipped a coin." Virgil smiled and put his hat back on. "I won."

Chapter Twenty

She was almost finished with her very good pie when another man with a badge walked in the door. Not as tall, somewhat slighter, but better dressed and very handsome. He looked around, spotted her and walked over. Now all the other diners watched, because this was the second man with a badge to visit her table.

"Miss Doyle?"

"Have a seat, Sherriff . . . Behan is it?"

He took his hat off and sat.

"I guess Marshal Earp told you I'd be coming in."

"He told me about the coin flip, yes."

"The Earps," he said, "they are more gamblers than lawmen."

"Then why did you flip the coin with him?"

"To illustrate that fact for you."

"And why would it matter to me?"

"Because big things are brewing in this town," he said. "We have the Earps, the Clantons, Johnny Ringo and Doc Holliday. We had Bat Masterson and Clint Adams for a while, but they left. But there's still plenty of firepower here to cause a ruckus."

"And you want to stop it? Or are you just waiting for it to happen so you can take sides?"

"My side will be the law's side, Ma'am," he said. "Like I told you, the Earps are gamblers, and they're also criminals."

"Why would a criminal be wearing a marshal's badge?"

"Well, they also have people fooled," he said.

"But not you?"

"No, not me and not Ike Clanton."

"Is he the head of these Clantons you mentioned?"

"He is. The Clantons are just some cowhands who like coming to town, but the Earps are determined to drive them away."

Roxy knew something else had to be going on here. It really didn't matter, though. She wasn't there to take sides."

"If you're going to ask me to pick a side—"

"That's not why I'm here," Behan said, cutting her off.

"Oh? Then why are we having this conversation?"

"I want you to leave town," he said.

"Why is that?"

"I told you, we have enough firepower here in Tombstone. We don't need to add the Lady Gunsmith to it."

"Then you have nothing to worry about," she said. "I'm not here to add my gun to anybody's side. I have some business of my own, and when that's done, I'll leave."

"I'm afraid I have to ask you to leave before then."

"How soon were you thinking?" she asked.

"Right after you finish that pie."

She looked at him, put the last piece of pie into her mouth, and chewed.

"I have no intention of leaving until my business is done," she said, after swallowing.

"Some people aren't going to like that."

"Like who?"

"Johnny Ringo, for one."

She sat back in her chair.

"You're trying to scare me with Johnny Ringo?"

"I'd think Ringo would scare anyone," he said, "who has half a brain."

"Are you trying to be offensive, Sheriff?"

"Not at all, Miss Doyle," he said. "I'm trying to save everybody a lot of trouble. You see, I know of your connection to the Gunsmith, and his connection to Wyatt Earp. Therefore—"

"—therefore you think there would be a connection between me and the Earps?"

"I do."

"Well, you couldn't be more wrong. In fact, Marshal Earp is the first one of the brothers I've ever met." She stood up, dropped her napkin on the table.

"Sheriff," she went on, "you haven't even asked me my business here in Tombstone, so I won't tell you. Just know that I'm not leaving until it's done, and you can't scare me away with Johnny Ringo, or anybody else."

Behan stood up, hat still in hand.

"I see I've played this wrong, Ma'am—"

"And don't call me Ma'am!"

She went to the waiter, paid her bill, and left the restaurant. She had intended to go into the saloon part of the Crystal Palace and have a drink, but she had already stormed out the door to make a point, and couldn't very well turn around and go back in. So she simply went off in search of 312 Fremont Street.

***

As Sheriff John Behan left the Crystal Palace, Virgil Earp appeared in front of him.

"Doesn't look like it went too well for you, Johnny," Virgil said.

"You and your brothers just better not be looking to recruit her, Marshal," Behan said.

"What makes you think we'd do that?" Virgil asked. "Or that we'd even need to."

"Just remember," Behan said, "and tell Wyatt not to try and trade on his friendship with the Gunsmith."

"If we were gonna do that, Sheriff," Virgil said, "don't you think we'd recruit the actual Gunsmith? And not a female version?"

Behan stormed away, angry with himself for having misplayed the entire matter.

Chapter Twenty-One

As Marshal Earp had told her, 312 Fremont Street was a two story boarding house that backed up to the O.K. Corral livery stable. There was a one story section on the back of the building that housed the Fly Photographic Gallery. Even though she'd been told that Fly was not in town, she knocked on the door there before going to the front of the house.

The door was answered by a woman in her early to mid-30's who, despite a tired look, gave Roxy a pleasant smile.

"I'm sorry," she said, "if you're lookin' for a room we're full up."

"I'm not looking for a room," Roxy said. "I'm looking for C.S. Fly."

"Buck?" the woman said. "He's away, but I'm Mollie Fly, his wife. Does this have something to do with the gallery out back?"

"Yes, it does."

Now Mollie Fly really smiled.

"I can help you there," she said. "You see, I'm also a photographer. Buck and I run this boarding house and the gallery together."

"All right, then," Roxy said. "Maybe you *can* help me. I'd like to—"

"Why don't you go around back to the door and I'll unlock it and let you in," Mollie said. "Just give me a minute."

"But I just need to—" Roxy asked, but the woman backed into the house and closed the door, cutting her off in mid-sentence.

She sighed, stepped down from the porch and went around to the back, again. As she waited for Mollie Fly to unlock the door she turned her head and looked over at the empty corral.

Then she heard the lock turn and the door opened. There was Mollie, once again smiling, but she seemed to have fixed her hair. At the front door much of it was hanging down in front of her face, but now it had been pulled back. Roxy could tell she'd be a pretty woman, with some care.

"Come in, come in," Mollie said. "I didn't get your name out front."

"I didn't give it," Roxy said. "It's Roxy Doyle."

Mollie froze for a moment, then closed the door. She stood there with her hand on it for a few seconds before turning and looking at Roxy.

"Doyle?"

"That's right," Roxy said. "Does that mean anything to you?"

"Well, no," Mollie said, "I can't say it does—"

"But you reacted when you heard the name," Roxy insisted. "My father is Gavin Doyle. I'm here because your husband took a photo of my father some time ago—"

"Who told you that?"

"William Benson," Roxy said. "He runs the Mathew Brady Gallery in Santa Fe. He has the photo there."

"He's a liar," Mollie said. "He doesn't work for Brady, anymore."

"I know," Roxy said. "He's just trying to play off Brady's name, but I don't care about that. I saw the photo, it's a portrait. I just need to talk to your husband—"

"My husband didn't know he was Gavin Doyle when he took the photo!" Mollie blurted. "If you're hunting Doyle to kill him, my husband can't help you."

"Kill him?" Roxy repeated. "He's my father. I only want to see him, talk to him."

Mollie frowned at Roxy.

"He really is your father?"

"Yes, he is."

Mollie stared inward for a short time, then said to Roxy, "Why don't you have a seat?"

Roxy looked around. There were two chairs in the gallery, so she pulled one up and sat in it. Mollie Fly remained standing, fidgeting.

"I told Buck he was lookin' for trouble," she said.

"How?"

"He kept sayin' how he was going to sell the photo for a lot of money."

"I suppose he might have, if he hadn't given it to Benson—" Roxy went on.

"But that's just it," Roxy said, cutting her off.

"What is?"

"Buck didn't give the photo to William," Mollie said. "Benson stole it."

"What?"

"That's right," Mollie said. "It was here, in the gallery, when we left to go take shots of some Comanches, and when we came back he was gone, and so was that photo."

Roxy thought about that for a moment. In the end, it didn't change anything for her.

"I know where the photo is now," she said. "If you want it back, you've got it. But I need to know what my father and your husband talked about. I need to know if he gave Buck any idea where he was going, or where he was living or going to live."

"I see."

"Do you know if he told your husband any of that?"

"Not that he mentioned to me."

"Then I have to talk to him," Roxy said. "When will he be back?"

"Within the next few days."

"Guess I'll have to stick around."

"Is that a problem for you?" Mollie asked.

"I've already been questioned by two lawmen," Roxy said. "One of them, Sheriff Behan, told me to leave."

"Johnny Behan's a fool," Mollie said. "He's friendly with those cowboys, the whole Clanton bunch, including Johnny Ringo, Curly Bill Brocius and the McLaury brothers, Tom and Frank."

"And on the other side?"

"That's easy," Mollie said. "The Earps, Wyatt, Morgan and Marshal Virgil, along with Doc Holliday."

"I've heard of them, and Johnny Ringo, but nobody else on the other side."

"They're local," she said," and they had no trouble plying their outlaw trade before the Earps came to town."

"How do you know so much about it?"

"Everybody in town knows about it," Mollie said. "We're all waitin' for the explosion that's comin'. There's gonna be blood in the streets, as well as dead men."

"Sounds like something worth photographing," Roxy said. "You know, in the name of history."

Mollie grinned. "Don't think I haven't thought about that. Are you intending to join one side?"

"I only have one side," Roxy said. "Mine. I'm going to do my business here and move on."

"And that business means talkin' to my husband."

"Right."

"All right," Mollie said. "I'll let you know when he gets back to town."

"I'd be much obliged." Roxy knew she'd hear when Buck Fly got back to town on her own, but thanked the woman, anyway.

"Where are you staying?" Mollie asked.

"The Grand Hotel."

"Nice place," Mollie said. "Wyatt and Doc are staying there."

"So I've been told."

Mollie walked Roxy to the door of the gallery.

"You could stay here, if you like. I'd give you a cheaper rate than the hotel."

"I'm good," Roxy said. "I came into some money a while back, and I'm still working on it."

"Suit yourself."

"I usually do," she said. "Thanks, Mollie."

"Come by again," Mollie said. "So you and I can talk. I like you, Roxy."

"I appreciate that, Mollie," Roxy said, and left without returning the sentiment. She may have liked the woman, but she wasn't about to admit it.

Not yet, anyway.

Chapter Twenty-Two

"You want Ringo to do what?" Ike Clanton asked.

"Scare her," Behan said. "Right out of town."

Clanton laughed, looked around the small saloon he and his family and men used in Tombstone as headquarters. Curly Bill Brocius and Ike's 19 year-old brother, Billy, still at the bar, and started to laugh.

"I'll do it," Curly Bill said. "I'll scare the pants off her, and then you know what I'll do? I'll—"

"Shut up, Curly Bill!" Clanton snapped.

Brocius shut his mouth, but he was still grinning.

"Do you know who this woman is, Johnny?" Clanton asked.

"Of course I do," Behan said. "I found out who she is. Roxy Doyle—"

"—Lady Gunsmith, right!" Clanton said, cutting him off. "We don't need her standing with the Earps when the time comes."

"Exactly why I want her out of town."

"Not scared out," Clanton said, "carried out. Right to boot hill."

"Ike—"

"If Johnny Ringo is gonna do anythin', it's kill her, not scare her."

"Ike—"

"I don't care if he puts a bullet in her back," Clanton went on. "I don't care how he does it, just so long as it gets done."

"Ike, I'm the law here. I'm not going to tell Johnny Ringo to kill somebody."

"You don't have to," Clanton said. "I'll take care of that. I'll send Tom and Frank to find him. This Lady Gunsmith will be dead by tomorrow night."

"I don't want to hear about it," Behan said.

"Don't be such a scared rabbit, Johnny," Billy Brocius said from the bar.

"Shut up, Billy," Ike Clanton and John Behan said, at the same time.

***

Virgil Earp entered the Bird Cage and saw his brother, Wyatt, taking a break from dealing Faro, at the bar. He joined him.

"Beer, Virg?" Wyatt asked.

"Definitely."

"Where's Morg?" Wyatt asked, as he waved to the bartender to give his brother a beer.

"He's workin'," Virgil said.

"Aren't you supposed to be workin'?" Wyatt asked.

"I am." Virgil grabbed his beer from the bar. "You know who Roxy Doyle is?"

"Roxy—yeah, didn't Clint tell us about her? Oh, wait, she's Lady Gunsmith, right?"

"Right," Virgil said. "She's in town."

"Lady Gunsmith is here?" Wyatt said. "Why?"

"She claims she's lookin' for her father."

"Whose her father?"

"Gavin Doyle?"

Wyatt paused with his beer halfway to his mouth and looked surprised.

"The bounty hunter?"

"One and the same."

"That's quite a family tree," Wyatt said. "And her mentor was the Gunsmith. I wonder how good she is?"

"What does that matter?"

"We could always use another gun," Wyatt said.

"We have another gun. Doc."

"You, me, Morg and Doc," Wyatt said. "We're a little outnumbered."

"We have right on our side," Virgil said. "Or have you forgotten?"

"Never," Wyatt said. "But we could've used Clint or Bat to stick around. So now we have a chance to recruit—"

"Wyatt," Virgil said, "this is our fight. I ain't lookin' to get nobody else killed."

"Speak of the devil," Wyatt said, looking past his brother.

Doc Holliday came across the Bird Cage floor, attracting attention as he went, and joined them at the bar. He was small and slighter than the two brothers, but anybody in the place would have said he was the most deadly.

"Beer?" Wyatt asked.

"On you?"

"Naturally."

"Always."

Wyatt waved at the bartender for three fresh ones.

When they each had one in their hands, Doc asked, "What did I interrupt. It looked like a family fight."

"Virgil was tellin' me that Roxy Doyle is in town," Wyatt said.

"That redhaired student of Clint Adams'? Lady Gun-smith?"

"The same," Virgil said.

"Oh, shit!" Doc swore, as if something had just occurred to him.

"What?"

"I met her."

"When?"

"Earlier today, in the hallway of our hotel," Doc said. "She came blastin' out of her room and just about knocked me sideways."

"She's in our hotel?"

Doc nodded. "And she's as beautiful as they say."

"Did she recognize you?" Wyatt asked.

"Naw," Doc said, "she barely looked at me. Fine lookin' woman."

"Don't let Kate hear you say that," Virgil said, referring to Doc's woman, Big-Nose Kate.

"Ah, Kate's in Globe, and she probably ain't comin' back."

"She'll be back," Virgil said. "She always comes back to you, Doc."

Doc said. "So what were you boys arguin' about?"

"Wyatt wants to recruit the lady," Virgil said. "I told him we don't need another gun. We got you."

Doc looked at Wyatt, who shrugged.

"I suppose you better recruit her," Doc said, "before Ike does."

"If she learned from Clint Adams," Virgil said, "there's no way Ike can get her. Besides, she's only here to find out somethin' about her father, Gavin Doyle."

"Doyle the bounty hunter?" Doc asked.

Virgil nodded.

"Shit, I thought he was dead."

Chapter Twenty-Three

Roxy had nothing to do until Buck Fly returned to town, so she decided to take a look at what Tombstone had to offer in the way of recreation. Marshal Earp had mentioned his brother dealing Faro at the Bird Cage, and since Wyatt Earp was a close friend of Clint Adams, she felt it only right to pay her respects.

As she entered the Bird Cage she saw it was a combination saloon and theater. The interior was impressive, with balconies around the room, from where the shows on stage could be watched. The main floor was peppered with gaming tables, and plenty of girls working the floor.

She saw Virgil Earp standing at the bar with two men. One she recognized as the man she bumped into in the hall of her hotel. The other resembled Virgil slightly, so she assumed he was Wyatt Earp.

She hadn't planned on approaching them, rather she figured to go to the bar and get a beer. Then she could stand there, drink it and look the place over. However, as she got close, Marshal Earp looked over at her and waved an invitation.

"Marshal," she said, as she reached them.

"Miss Doyle, I want you to meet my brother, Wyatt," Virgil said.

She nodded to Wyatt Earp. "Any friend of Clint's is a friend of mine."

"I feel the same way," he said, and shook her hand.

"And this gent, who says you just about knocked him over at the hotel this mornin', is Doc Holliday."

"Well," she said, "if I'd known it was you, I would've been a lot more careful." They shook hands, as well.

"Don't give it a second thought," Doc said. "It was my pleasure."

"Would you have a beer with us?" Virgil asked.

"I'd be happy to."

This time it was Virgil motioning to the bartender for a beer. When it came he picked it up and handed it to Roxy.

"Thank you."

"Have you concluded your business in town?" Virgil asked.

She sipped her beer and said, "Not even close. I think you may have mentioned to me that Mr. Fly was not in town, and you were right. I spoke with his wife, though, and she assures me he'll be back any day."

"So you plan to wait?" Virgil asked.

"I do," she said. "There's no point in coming all this way from New Mexico to just leave without talking to him."

"Makes sense to me," Doc said. "How do you intend to spend your time? Do you play poker?"

"I'm afraid I don't play poker or Faro," she said. "I'll just have to find other ways to pass the time."

"Well," Virgil said, "this is Tombstone. There isn't a lot to do."

"I'll manage," she said.

"Please excuse me," Doc Holliday said, "if you don't mind, I'm gonna go and find a poker game."

"Good luck, Doc," Wyatt said. "Try not to get into the same game as Ringo."

"Why not?" Doc said. "I'll take all that jasper's money with a smile. Miss Doyle."

"Mr. Holliday."

"Oh, no, no," he said, "you just call me Doc."

"All right," she said, "and I'm Roxy."

"See you later, Roxy."

Doc finished his beer, coughed a bit into his handkerchief, and took his leave.

"I noticed he was coughing at the hotel," she said. "I think that's why he ran into me."

"Funny," Wyatt said, "he said you ran into him."

She laughed. "It was probably a combination. But is he all right?"

"No," Wyatt said, "Doc's very sick, although we're not really sure with what. You can see how slight he is, he's lost a lot of weight, and been coughing up blood."

"Consumption?" she asked.

"Probably," Wyatt said. "He came west for the weather, but it hasn't seemed to help."

"I'm sorry to hear that."

Virgil finished his beer and set the empty mug down on the bar.

"I've got to get back to work," he said. "Miss Do—Roxy. I hope you find some entertainment."

"Thank you, Marshal."

Virgil walked away, leaving Roxy alone with Wyatt Earp.

"Clint's told me you're the most natural talent with a gun he's ever seen."

"Really? He didn't tell me that."

"Well, he thought enough of you to spend all that time training you."

"Yes," she said, "but he was very stingy with the compliments, so I'm glad to hear it from you."

"And Virgil tells me Gavin Doyle is your father."

"Yes, that's right."

"He's got quite a reputation as a bounty hunter."

"That's about all I know," she said. "I haven't seen him since I was ten or eleven."

"How do you expect to recognize him?" Wyatt asked.

"Well," Roxy said, "I was wondering that too, until just recently, when I saw . . ."

Chapter Twenty-Four

Johnny Ringo walked into the Silver Spur Saloon, saw Ike Clanton sitting at a table alone. At the bar were Tom and Frank McLaury, along with Curly Bill Brocius. Some of the other tables were taken, but it was a small, out of the way saloon that didn't do much business. That was why Ike liked it. Ringo walked to Ike's table.

"I hear you're lookn' for me," he said.

"Have a seat, Johnny." Ike looked at the bar. "Billy, bring Johnny a beer!"

"Sure, Ike," his brother said.

Billy Clanton grabbed a beer from the bar and carried it to the table. He set it down in front of Ringo, then went back to the bar.

Ringo took a deep pull on the beer then asked, "What's on your mind, Ike?"

"Roxy Doyle."

"Who's that?"

"Otherwise known as Lady Gunsmith."

Ringo wiped his mouth with the back of his hand.

"Is she for real?" he asked.

"Looks like it," Ike said. "And she's in town."

"Is Clint Adams with 'er?" Ringo asked. "I'd like to try him."

Ringo wasn't in town when the Gunsmith was there a few weeks back.

"No, he ain't here. Just her."

"So whataya need me for?"

"If you kill her," Ike said, "maybe that'll being Adams back, and you can have your try."

"Kill a woman?" Ringo asked.

"Does that bother you?" Ike asked. "From her reputation, she's killed plenty of men."

"Why do you want her dead?" Ringo asked.

"Because I don't want her adding her gun to the Earps' and Doc Holliday's, that's why."

"So where is she?" he asked.

"In town, somewhere," Ike said. "Sheriff Behan says you can't miss her. She has a lot of red hair and a better body than any saloon girl you've ever seen."

"And you want me to kill her?" Ringo said.

"Do whatever you want with her," Ike said, "but after that, get rid of her."

"Seems like a shame," Ringo said.

"We have enough to deal with," Ike said.

"Yeah, yeah, I know," Ringo said, "but when do I get the chance to kill Doc?"

"That's comin'," Ike Clanton told him. "I promise. The time is comin' for Holliday, and the Earps."

Ringo finished his beer and stood up.

"I think I'll take a walk around town," he said, "and see if I can find me some red hair."

"Let me know when it's done."

***

106

Wyatt Earp excused himself to go back to his Faro table, and Roxy ordered herself another beer. Then she did what she had been planning to do, stood with her back to the bar and gave the place a good look.

The stage was bare, and as a result, so were the balconies. There was plenty going on down below, though, as men gambled and grabbed at the girls who were working the floor, serving drinks and going downstairs with a man when the job called for it. Most places Roxy had been had rooms upstairs for the girls to take their customers, but the Bird Cage obviously had the rooms downstairs.

Most of the girls she could see were very pretty, of all ages and sizes, so that there was something for every man's taste.

And possibly every woman's.

One of the saloon girls came over and stood next to her. She was young, pretty, dressed in a ruby colored gown, with long black hair that fell to her creamy, smooth white shoulders. Her nails were colored to match the dress. Roxy had never colored her nails.

"I hope you're not thinkin' of workin' here," the girl said.

"Why not?" Roxy asked.

"Well, Jesus, you're so beautiful," the girl said. "None of the rest of us would have a chance."

"Relax," Roxy said, "I'm not looking for a job. I'm just passing the time."

The girl turned and faced Roxy. She was a couple of inches shorter, so she looked up, slightly. Roxy noticed her eyes were a deep blue.

"Would you like to pass it with me?" she asked. "I have a room downstairs."

"Excuse me," Roxy said, "but isn't that where you're supposed to take your male customers?

The girl smiled. "I can take anybody I like. Anybody I take a fancy to." She wet her lips with her tongue, a gesture Roxy was sure worked on most men. The girl had luscious, full lips. 'What's your name?"

"Roxy."

"I'm Maggie. So, whataya say?"

The girl reached out and ran her finger down Roxy's arm, a suggestive, flirty look on her face.

Roxy had been approached by women before. In the beginning, when she was younger, it would embarrass her. Now that she was more experienced, she invariably found it flattering.

"Maggie," she said, "it's a tempting offer, it really is, but you see, I prefer men—exclusively."

"Too bad, really," Maggie said. "A couple of the other girls were curious, also. Should I tell them not to bother trying? Or is it just me?"

"No, it's not just you," Roxy said, "you're beautiful. And yes, tell them not to bother trying."

"Well, okay," Maggie said, reluctant to move away, "but if you ever change your mind, remember—"

"—Maggie," Roxy said. "I'll remember."

Maggie shook her head and said, "God, you're so damn beautiful."

She moved away finally, disappearing into the innards of the Bird Cage.

Chapter Twenty-Five

Johnny Ringo hit several of Tombstone's saloons—The Bucket of Blood, the Bella Union, the Oriental, the Crystal Palace, with no sign of a redhead wearing a gun. However, at the Crystal Palace he did hear she had been there, eating.

That left the Bird Cage.

Ike Clanton wanted all the cowboys, and Johnny Ringo, to stay away from the Bird Cage. Walking in there would put them in direct contact with Wyatt Earp and Doc Holliday.

The presence of Doc Holliday was like catnip to Johnny Ringo, though. He'd like nothing better than to go up against Holliday with his gun. But as long as he was on Ike Clanton's payroll, he had to toe the line Ike drew in the sand. The man was biding his time before going up against the Earps.

The odd thing was that while Ringo hated Doc Holliday, he had nothing against Wyatt Earp. If he went into the Bird Cage he might end up having to kill Wyatt, and he wouldn't like that.

Not yet, anyway.

He decided to wait outside the Bird Cage and see if the redhead went in or came out. And if Doc came out and saw him, even better.

***

Roxy was pleased to have met the three men, who were friends—to one degree or another—of Clint Adams. She knew there were also other Earp brothers in town and wondered if she'd get the opportunity to meet them, as well. It was a legendary family.

And she was surprised at how pleased she was they had heard of her. She had no idea how much or how little Clint spoke of her to other people. If this was any indication, then he only had good things to say.

She finished her second beer and decided not to have a third. She'd been riding all day and was starting to feel the effects. She was disappointed that Fly was out of town but in waiting for him she'd be able to get some rest. Her horse could use the time, as well.

She left the Bird Cage without exchanging further words with Wyatt Earp or Doc Holliday, who were both busy with their cards.

***

Johnny Ringo saw the redhaired woman come out of the Bird Cage and found himself staring as she walked down the street. He'd had many women in his time, whores, saloon girls, but he'd never seen a woman like this. By the time he realized he needed to follow her, she was a block away. He stepped out of his doorway and started after her.

***

Roxy saw the tall, thin man in the doorway across the street, felt he was watching her, but paid him no mind. She was used to men watching her. But when she realized he was following her, she knew there was something more to it.

She turned off of Allen Street and stepped into an alley between a bakery and a leather shop. As the man went hurrying by, trying to see where she'd gone, she stepped out behind him.

"Looking for me?" she called.

He turned quickly, reaching for his gun. Roxy did something Clint Adams had always told her not to do. She drew her gun but didn't fire it. Beaten to the draw, Ringo froze.

"Let's leave that gun where it is, shall we?" she asked.

"What's your beef?" Ringo asked.

"Why are you following me?"

"What makes you think I got nothin' better to do than follow you?"

"I saw you across from the Bird Cage when I came out," she said, "and here you are, right behind me."

"You got a real high opinion of yourself, lady," Ringo said. "I ain't following you."

"Well, good," she said, "then I won't have to worry about seeing you again."

"We're both in this town," he told her. "You'll see me again. And it'll go different next time."

"Think so?" She holstered her gun. "Go ahead, show me."

"Huh-uh," Johnny Ringo said. "When I'm good and ready."

"Your call," she said.

She backed away until she got to Allen Street, then turned and started walking.

Johnny Ringo stayed where he was. He was impressed that Lady Gunsmith was as beautiful as they said she was but dismayed that she was as fast as she was. But he convinced himself that she had gotten the drop on him, and it would go differently next time.

And there would be a next time.

***

Roxy had no idea who the man was, but he was obviously a gunman. The way he'd been ready to draw when he turned indicated that. She knew Clint Adams would have given her hell for drawing and not firing her gun, but something had told her to hold back.

He could only have been following her for one of two reasons—to rape her or kill her. With that thought she wondered why she hadn't killed him?

She only hoped the decision wouldn't come back to haunt her.

Chapter Twenty-Six

Roxy stayed in her room the rest of the night and woke well rested. Mollie Fly said her husband would be home any day, but Roxy now figured she wouldn't be lucky enough to have him show up so soon after her arrival.

She had already been told by two lawmen that Tombstone was a powderkeg, and it was already her experience, in her fairly young life, that she didn't fare well in these kinds of towns. Somehow, she usually got involved in lighting the fuse.

Well, not this time. She was determined not to take sides. She was going to wait to see Buck Fly, find out what she wanted about her father, and then leave Tombstone to light its own fuse.

She went down to the lobby, looked into the hotel dining room and found it only half full. There were tables against the rear wall, which was just what she wanted.

"Ma'am?" a young male waiter said. "Joinin' us for breakfast this mornin'?"

"Yes, I am."

"Well, pick a table," he said.

"Thanks."

She walked to one in the back tables, with the waiter following her.

"What have you got this morning?" she asked, as she sat.

"Whatever you want," he said. "Flapjacks, biscuits, ham-and-eggs, steak-and-eggs—you want somethin' else you let me know, and I'll have the cook make it for you."

She wondered if all the other guests got the same offer.

"I'll settle for the ham-and-eggs," she said, "with biscuits and coffee."

"Comin' up!"

The young waiter rushed to the kitchen to put in her order, then rushed back with a basket of biscuits, some butter and honey, and her coffee.

"Why didn't we get service like that?" a middle-aged woman asked her husband.

He didn't answer her. It would only have made her madder, and she was mad enough that he had been looking at the redhaired woman since she walked in.

Roxy put some butter and honey on a hot biscuit, ate it and washed it down with the good, hot coffee. By then the waiter returned with her ham-and-eggs.

"Thanks."

"Let me know if you want anything else," the waiter said.

"I will."

But she didn't. She had plenty of food and coffee, and when she was done she paid the man and thanked him. As she left the man and his wife watched her go, he with admiration, and she with annoyance at the quick service Roxy had gotten.

Outside Roxy stopped and took in a deep breath—or as deep as she could. The air was hot and still, and it was only going to get hotter.

***

Doc Holliday combed his hair that morning, then spent a few minutes sitting out a coughing fit, which brought out not blood, but a yellowish liquid. He didn't know which was worse, this or the blood. He washed out his mouth, put on his black jacket and hat, and left the room.

In the lobby he spotted Roxy Doyle coming out of the dining room and leaving the hotel. When he saw her stop outside the door, he hurried to catch up.

"Looks like I missed havin' breakfast with a pretty lady," he said, coming up alongside of her.

"Oh, good morning," she said. "Yeah, I guess I get up pretty early."

"Too bad," he said, "it would have given us time to get acquainted."

"Maybe you can help me with something, Doc," she said. I'll come in and have some coffee while you eat."

"Splendid!"

They went inside and were seated at another back table. Roxy liked Doc's slight Southern accent, and his Southern manners. All she knew about him was his reputation as a vicious killer. Maybe getting acquainted wouldn't be such a bad idea. And there *was* something she wanted to ask him.

Doc ordered flapjacks while the waiter poured them both some coffee.

"Doc, Wyatt told me about your condition," Roxy said. "I'm so sorry to hear it."

"Don't be sorry, my dear," he said. "There's nothin' anybody can do about it. What will be, will be. I know a bit about you, also—although it's third hand. Wyatt told me what Clint told him."

"I wonder how accurate it was by the time it got to you?" she said, laughing.

"Well, they said you were beautiful," he said. "At least that's accurate."

Roxy laughed again and said, "Thanks." For some reason, his compliment didn't sound as smarmy as it did coming from other men.

"Doc, I was followed by a man last night when I left the Bird Cage."

"Seems to me someone like you would be followed by men a lot—and I don't mean just because of how you look."

"Well, this one had something about him—something dangerous. I should've killed him, but I didn't."

"And now you're havin' second thoughts?"

"Yes."

"What did he look like?"

As she described the man she saw a look of recognition come into Doc's eyes. He put his fork down and looked across the table at her.

"Did he draw on you?"

"He didn't have time. I got the drop on him."

"You beat him to the draw?" he asked, his eyes widening.

"Well, I came up behind him. He started to go for his gun as he turned but, yeah, I beat 'im."

"I don't know if even I could do that," Doc admitted.

"Really? Who is he?"

"Johnny Ringo."

"Ringo?"

"You were right about him bein' dangerous—and add vicious."

"I guess I got lucky," she said.

"But you should've killed him," Doc said. "Johnny's not about to let that go."

"Damn it," she said. "I was hoping to stay out of trouble here until I finished my business."

"Well, it's not only Ringo," he said. "If Johnny's got it in for you, then so do the Clantons and the cowboys. That means the McLaurys, Curly Bill, and the lot of 'em. Not to mention Sheriff Behan."

"So in spite of it all," she said, "I've taken sides."

He picked his fork up again, speared a hunk of flapjacks and said, "Looks like it."

Chapter Twenty-Seven

Roxy thanked Doc and left him to his breakfast, despite his protests.

Outside once again she stopped and looked around. She didn't see Johnny Ringo anywhere. She had heard of Ringo, heard he was deadly with a gun. Since her time with Clint Adams, and as Lady Gunsmith, she had come up against only a handful of gun-toters with legitimate reputations. Johnny Ringo was now one of them. So far she had been lucky enough—good enough, Clint would say—to walk away alive.

From what Doc Holliday had said about Ringo, she had a feeling the man could end up being her biggest test.

She decided to try to do something to avoid it. She stepped off the boardwalk and headed for the sheriff's office.

***

Sheriff John Behan was in his office when she entered, pouring some whiskey into a cup of coffee.

"Keeps what ails you away," he said, putting the bottle away and sitting at his desk. "What can I do for you this morning, Miss Doyle?"

"You can tell Johnny Ringo to stay away from me," she told him. "I'm not looking for any trouble, Sheriff."

"Ringo," he said, shaking his head. "I don't have much control over him. And unlike you, he's always looking for trouble."

"Well, if he pushes me he's going to find it."

"What did he do?"

"He followed me, yesterday," she said. "I don't like being trailed."

"You talk to him about it?"

"I did," she said. "I beat him to the draw, and he didn't like it."

"Wait a minute," Behan said. "You beat Ringo, and he's not dead?"

"I didn't kill him," she said. "I didn't know who he was when I drew on him."

"Oh, Miss Doyle," he said, "you do have a problem. If you beat Ringo to the draw once, he's going to want to test you again. And since you didn't kill him the first time, he's going to figure he has the upper hand. That you don't have the killer instinct."

"He'll find out he's wrong if he comes after me," she said. "Tell him that for me."

Behan shook his head and chuckled.

"You picked the baddest man in town to get mad at you," he told her. "About the only one who might've been worse is Doc Holliday."

"Doc and I are getting along fine."

"Well, good for you," he said. "Maybe you can get him to help you with Ringo. Those two are like oil and water, they just don't like each other."

"I don't need Doc Holliday," she said. "If Ringo wants to push me I'll take care of it myself."

"So where do I come in?"

"You're the law," she said.

"Virgil Earp is the marshal," Behan pointed out. "Why don't you ask him?"

"Because you're connected with Ike Clanton and his men, and Ringo is one of those men."

"I can guess who you've been talking to," Behan said. "The Earps. I have no connection with Clanton and his Cowboys. And I sure as hell have no influence over Johnny Ringo."

"Just remember I came to talk to you," she said, "trying to avoid trouble. But you seem to have enough brewing without me adding to it."

"You remember what I said," Behan said. "Ringo isn't going to go away."

"If he comes after me," she said, "he's going away forever!"

Chapter Twenty-Eight

Roxy figured talking to Sheriff Behan had done her no good. Maybe the man was right. Maybe she should be talking to the other lawman in town, Marshal Virgil Earp.

She found the marshal's office and went inside. The man behind the desk wasn't Virgil, but it looked a little like him. He was wearing a deputy marshal's badge.

"Can I help ya?" he asked.

"I was looking for Marshal Earp," she said.

"Well," he said, with a smile, "I'm Deputy Marshal Earp."

"A brother?"

"I'm Morgan. You must be Miss Doyle."

"That's right."

"Virgil and Wyatt told me you were in town," Morgan said. "Was Virgil expecting you this morning?"

"No," she said, "I just wanted to ask him about something."

"Maybe I can help."

"Do you know Johnny Ringo?"

"Everybody in Tombstone knows Ringo," he said. "Why?"

She told him what she had already told Doc Holliday and Sheriff Behan.

"Behan wasn't much help, huh?" he asked, when she was done.

"None at all," she admitted.

"So you thought maybe Virgil could talk to Ringo? Get him to back off?"

"I was just going to ask."

"I'm afraid Ringo would just love for one of us to try to get him to do something he doesn't want to," Morgan said. "Somebody would end up dead."

"He's that bad? He'd draw on a U.S. marshal?"

"He would," Morgan said. "although he'd much rather draw on Doc—or now, maybe you."

"This is ridiculous," she said. "I didn't come here looking for trouble."

"Well, you might be able to avoid him," Morgan said. "Stay inside until you finish your business."

"Did your brothers tell you what my business was?" she asked.

"You want to talk to the photographer, Fly."

"Right."

"Maybe Mollie can send word to your hotel when he gets back," Morgan suggested.

"So I should just hide in my hotel until then?"

"Only if you want to avoid Ringo."

"I want to avoid him," she said, "but not run or hide from him."

"Well then, I have another suggestion."

"What's that?"

"Stay with us."

"Pardon me?"

"I don't mean move in with us," he said. "I mean spend your days here, at the office, and when you have to leave, walk with one of us. See, Ike Clanton has told his men to keep away from us until he's good and ready."

"So if I'm always with you, or Virgil, or Wyatt—"

"—or Doc—"

"—they'll be staying away from me, too."

"Seems like it."

"Even Ringo?"

"If Ringo takes orders from anybody," Morgan said, "he takes 'em from Ike. But he also goes off half-cocked plenty of times. I'm just suggestin' somethin' that might help."

"I appreciate you taking the time to talk to me, deputy."

"Just call me Morg," he said. "Everybody does."

"You can call me Roxy while I'm here," she said. "I'm going to take what you said into consideration, so I may just be back here."

"I'll tell Wyatt and Virg," Morgan promised. "What about Doc?"

"I spoke to Doc this morning," she said. "He understands what's going on."

"Okay, then," Morgan said. "Maybe we'll be seein' you later."

Roxy nodded, and left the office.

Morgan sat back in his chair, shook his head in wonder. Clint Adams had said she was beautiful, but he'd understated the truth.

***

"You what?" Ike asked Ringo.

"Can't do it," Ringo said.

"Can't do what?"

"Kill that woman."

"Why not?" Ike asked. "Is she too damn fast for you, Johnny?"

Ringo looked at Ike Clanton, who was eating breakfast in a small restaurant off of Allen Street. They had offered Ringo a plate or some coffee when he entered, but he declined. Now he regarded Ike with some amusement.

"You're tryin' to get my goat, Ike," he said. "You know ain't nobody too fast for me."

"Then what is it?"

"Damn, Ike," Johnny Ringo said, "she's just too pretty to kill."

Chapter Twenty-Nine

From what Johnny Ringo told Ike Clanton of his encounter with the Lady Gunsmith, Ike was almost convinced it would drive her into the Earp fold. So if Ringo wouldn't kill her, he'd have to get somebody else to do it. But he couldn't use any of his own people. For one thing Curly Bill and the McLaury boys would never be able to stand up to her. They weren't fast guns. And if something went wrong, he could have walked away from Johnny Ringo. But if his other men were caught he was sure to be implicated. John Behan wouldn't try to arrest him, but Virgil Earp was just looking for an excuse.

That meant Ike had to import some talent to take care of Roxy Doyle.

Ike looked across the room, where Billy Clanton sat eating with the McLaury's, Tom and Frank.

"Billy!"

The 19 year-old, who idolized his 16 years older brother, jumped up from his chair and ran over.

"Yeah, Ike?"

"Siddown."

Billy could see Ike was in a foul mood, so he just waited.

"You gotta find Frank." Ike was referring to "Buckskin" Frank Leslie who, while he was a member of The Cowboys, was not willing to use his gun whenever Ike wanted him to.

"Okay!" Billy started to get up.

"Hold on, there!" Ike said. "I ain't finished."

Billy settled back down.

"Frank's got to find me three guns," Ike said, "who ain't particular when it comes to killin'."

"What about Ringo?"

"Seems like, suddenly, he's particular."

"What about Frank, hisself?"

"No," Ike said, "he wouldn't do it, either. In fact, I don't think Frank's gonna be around much longer. But before he goes, needs to find me those men."

"Okay."

"I want 'em as soon as possible."

"Right."

Billy sat still, and Ike glared at him.

"Now, Billy!" he snapped.

"Right, Ike!"

Billy stood up and ran out of the cafe. The McLaury brothers saw him go, grabbed his plate and divvied up the rest of his food.

***

When Roxy left the marshal's office she was at a loss for what to do with her time. She figured to stay out of saloons, for a while. And besides, it was too early for them to be open. She remembered that Mollie Fly had told her to come back, some time. She decided to go and spend time talking with the woman. Maybe she knew something she didn't realize she knew, and it would come out in conversation.

***

"I'm so glad you came by," Mollie Fly said, when she brought a tray of tea and cookies from her kitchen. "You'd think a woman who runs a boarding house would have somebody to talk to all day, but I don't."

"I'm happy to be here," Roxy said. "Tombstone can be pretty lonely, too, when you're trying to avoid people."

Mollie handed her a cup of tea.

"Oh? Who are you trying to avoid?"

"Well," Roxy said, "in general I'm trying to avoid trouble, but in particular I'm now trying to avoid Johnny Ringo."

"Ringo!" Mollie said, spitting the name out like a dirty word. "What a terrible man."

"That's what I heard."

"What did he do to you?"

"He was following me."

Mollie's eyes widened.

"What happened?"

"I convinced him not to follow me, anymore."

Mollie's eyes widened even more.

"How'd you do that?"

"I just showed him he's not so scary," Roxy said. "What experiences have you had with him?"

"With Johnny Ringo? None, and I don't want any. It's just that everybody in Tombstone gets out of the way of men like Ringo and Doc Holliday."

"What about the Earps?"

"Well, my husband has taken some photographs of Virgil, after he was named Marshal," Mollie said, "but we really don't have anythin' to do with them, either."

"So what do you do while your husband's away?" Roxy asked.

For the next half hour, over tea and cookies, the two women got acquainted. Roxy heard more about Mollie being a photographer in her own right, as well as running the boarding house. Mollie discovered that Roxy had left home at the age of 15 years ago and had been trying to find her father since then.

"So how many guests do you have here?" Roxy asked.

"A full house right now, but that don't happen often, I can tell you that," Mollie said. "We could use some more paying guests. Maybe then Buck wouldn't have to travel so much."

Now Roxy felt bad for having turned down Mollie's invitation to come and stay. She figured the woman hadn't been inviting her to stay for free, but now she knew they needed more paying customers.

"I'm not tryin' to make you feel guilty for stayin' at the hotel," Mollie hurriedly said. "You deserve to be comfortable. Have you run into the Earps or Doc Holliday there?"

"I literally ran into Doc in the hall yesterday," Roxy said. "Since then I've met and talked to all of them."

"This whole town is wondering when they and the Cowboys are gonna clash," Mollie said. "When they do, there's gonna be lots of blood and lead."

"Well, I don't want any part of that," Roxy said. "I'm just hoping your husband gets home before then, and I can complete my business."

"Find out about your father photograph," Mollie said.

"That's right."

"Well," Mollie said, "I know your father was here, and Buck took his photo. But I wasn't in the gallery when he did it, so I don't have any idea what they talked about."

"I believe you, Mollie," Roxy said.

"I just hope Buck will be able to tell you somethin' helpful," Mollie said.

"So do I." Roxy stood. "Thanks for the tea."

"Thanks for comin' by," Mollie said. "Let's do this again."

"Deal," Roxy said.

Chapter Thirty

It was late afternoon when Roxy walked down the street toward her hotel. She noticed how quiet it was, as if the people in town knew trouble was brewing. But was the street this quiet all the time? Or was it only because she was walking there?

Her eyes scanned the rooftops above her on either side, and the windows overlooking the street. Lastly, the doorways both ahead of her, and behind. There was no sign of Johnny Ringo, or any gunman.

Abruptly, she changed direction, and instead of going to her hotel, she walked to the Bird Cage and entered. It was noisy inside, but got quiet when the drinkers, gamblers and revelers noticed her.

Now she was sure the street was deserted because of her.

"There you are," Virgil Earp said, coming up next to her.

"Marshal."

"Where've you been?"

"I've been having tea and cookies with Mollie Fly. What's going on?"

"Word's gone around that you're going to be killed," Virgil said.

"By who? Ringo?"

"No, that's just it," Virgil said. "Nothin's been said about Ringo."

"Then who?"

"We don't know, exactly," Virgil said.

"How did you hear about this plan?" she asked.

"We've got eyes and ears all over town," Virgil said. "The word we got is that Ringo doesn't want to kill you, so Ike Clanton is findin' somebody else to do the job. Could be anybody. How about a beer while we talk about it?"

"Sure," she said, "lead the way."

As she followed Marshal Earp across the floor to the bar, she noticed Wyatt Earp dealing Faro, and Doc Holliday seated at a poker table.

"Two beers," Virgil told the bartender.

Slowly, the noise started up again, loud voices, and a piano from next to the stage.

Virgil handed Roxy a beer.

"Thanks." She took a drink. "If you know Ike Clanton's going to try to have me killed, why don't you arrest him?"

"I don't have proof," Virgil said. "It's just what we heard, me and Morgan. And besides, I can't arrest him for threatening to do somethin'."

"And who did you hear this from?

"Somebody who wouldn't testify."

"Your eyes and ears."

"Right."

"Well," she said, "apparently the whole towns heard it. The street's empty, and it got quiet in here when I came in."

"I get the feelin' you have that effect on any saloon when you come in."

"Marshal," she said, "are you being charming?"

"Ask my wife," he said. "I'm never charmin'."

"Do you think this is going to happen today?" she asked. "The attempt to kill me?"

"Probably not," Virgil said. "If the town knows, then Ike'll figure you know, too. No, they'll try to catch you off guard."

"I'll be careful."

"Morg told me what he suggested to you," Virgil said. "That you stay around us."

"I might end up getting one of you killed, instead of me," she said. "I can't do that, but I appreciate the offer."

"Well, now," Virgil said, "there just might be another way."

"What's that?"

"Doc," he said. "Nobody's gonna try to shoot you if you're with Doc."

"And what do you mean by 'with Doc?'" she asked.

"Ohm" he said, and it was funny to see Virgil Earp blush, "I didn't mean—"

"Never mind," she said. "I was just kidding. I understand. If I stay close to Doc, I should be all right."

"That's what I meant."

"How would Doc feel about that?"

"Having a beautiful woman close on his heels?" Virgil said. "Why would any man complain?"

"I thought I heard somewhere that he had a woman," she commented. "How would she feel?"

"Kate's not around, right now," Virgil said. "And we don't know if she'll ever be back, so I think you'd be safe there, too."

"I'll give it some thought," she said. "If someone's looking for me, I don't make it a habit of hiding."

"That works if they're comin' at you face-to-face. I just don't want you gettin' shot in the back."

"Believe me, Marshal," she responded, "I don't want that, either."

Chapter Thirty-One

As it turned out, Roxy didn't have to make a decision about approaching Doc Holliday, because Doc took a break from his game and came over to the bar.

"Beer," he told the bartender.

"Comin' up, Doc."

"Another for either of you?" the dentist turned gun-fighter/gambler asked.

"No, thanks, Doc," Virgil said. "I've got to get back to work. But perhaps the lady?"

"Sure, why not? Thank you, Doc."

The bartender brought over two fresh beers, and Doc handed Roxy hers as Virgil left the Bird Cage.

"Did Virgil fill you in on the word that's goin' around town?" Doc asked.

"You mean about somebody trying to kill me? He did, but you know as well as I do, Doc, that's not news. You and me, we've always got that kind of danger behind us."

"Too true, my dear," Doc said. "I just want to let you know, you can count on me for back-up, if it comes to that."

"I appreciate that, Doc."

Doc Holliday drained his mug and set the empty down on the bar.

"Meanwhile, I still have a game goin' on, if you'll excuse me."

"Of course."

Roxy watched as Doc went back to his table. She looked over at Wyatt Earp's Faro table, and he gave her a slight nod, which she returned. She was glad to be getting along with men who Clint Adams called his friends. She knew men of that caliber had egos, but at least for the moment, none seemed threatened in the least by a woman with a gun.

The one thing Clint Adams had not mentored Roxy Doyle in was gambling. She had not been able to muster up any interest in spending time sitting at a table when she could be out looking for her father.

Gambling would have to wait until later in life, when she was older and looking to sit in a chair for a long time.

As she headed for the door, unsure of her next move, Deputy Marshal Morgan Earp came through the batwing doors.

"Deputy," Roxy said. "If you're looking for the Marshal he was just here."

"Actually, I'm lookin' for you, Miss Doyle."

"Me? What for?"

"I just saw Buck Fly ride into town," he said. "Thought you'd like to know."

"He's back!" she said. "Finally."

"I'd just give him a chance to unhitch his team and get back home, maybe have a meal before I went chargin' in," Morgan suggested. "I'm just sayin'."

"Good advice," she said. "I'll give him a couple of hours. Thanks for the word."

"Hey," he said, "just tryin' to help. Buy you a beer?"

"No," she said, "but let me buy you one."

He smiled.

136

"Never turn down a free beer, that's what I always say."

Chapter Thirty-Two

"Who came looking for me?" Buck Fly asked his wife.

"Roxy Doyle."

Fly looked confused.

"Am I supposed to know who she is?" he asked. "Mollie, you don't think I have a girlfriend, do you?"

"Don't be ridiculous, Buck," she said. "I trust you."

He frowned. He was tired, hungry, and all his camera equipment was on the floor at his feet. Yet her attitude bothered him.

"Or don't you think I could get a girlfriend?" he asked. "Because I could, you know."

Mollie loved her husband. He wasn't handsome, but pleasant looking, if a little on the thin side. Still, he suited her and he would probably suit other women, as well.

"Of course you could, but she wasn't here for that, dear," Mollie said.

"Then what was she here for?"

"She's Gavin Doyle's daughter."

"Gavin—you mean, she *claims* to be Gavin Doyle's daughter."

"No, everyone in town—including the Earps—have accepted her as Roxy Doyle, Lady Gunsmith."

Fly dry washed his face with both hands, then said, "I need a bath, a meal and a drink, and then I can deal with this. Why is she here, anyway?"

"She's looking for her father and wants to ask you some questions."

"Well, I don't know what I'll be able to tell 'er," Fly said, "but let me start with that bath, and we'll go on from there."

"I'll make you something to eat," she said, "and then I can tell you what I know about her."

"How do you know anythin' about her?" he asked.

"We've talked more than once."

"Mollie," he said, "maybe we better start with you telling me what you've told her."

***

Roxy had a beer with Morgan Earp, even though she was itching to leave and go to the home of Mollie and Buck Fly.

"You look like you've got ants . . . crawling up your back," Morgan said. He was going to say "ants in your pants," but thought better of it, since Roxy was a lady.

"It shows, huh?" she asked.

"Look, Fly's gonna at least need a bath, and probably a meal. I think if you wait two hours, that should be enough."

"I guess," she said

"Look on the bright side."

"And where's that?"

"It's almost been a half hour already since I saw him drive his wagon in."

"You're right," she said. "I can wait another hour-and-a-half."

"Another beer?" he asked.

"I think I'll just have a cup of coffee, this time."

"Comin' up!" Morgan said.

***

"You sure she's inside?" Slade asked Booker.

"I told you," Booker said, "I saw her go in, myself. And I saw Marshal Earp leave."

"Yeah," Anderson said, "but that's the place where Wyatt and Doc deal."

"So what?" Booker asked. "We're gonna wait for her to come out. We ain't goin' in after her."

"He's right," Alex Slade said. "We'll just wait out here. Besides, Ike wants it done in public."

"And that's why we ain't bushwhackin' her—which makes a lot more sense to me," Ted Anderson said.

"I know," Booker said. "But shootin' her in the back would be so much easier."

"We ain't shootin' her in the back," Slade said.

Slade was 35 and had been making his way with a gun since he was 20. Shootin' a man—or a woman—in the back didn't sit right with him. After all, he wouldn't want to be killed that way. He'd want to face his killer, and he thought everybody deserved that chance.

On the other hand, Ted Anderson and Bobby Booker had shot many men in the back and never flinched. But they didn't have Slade's ability, or confidence, with a gun. Facing your target, there was just too much chance of getting killed.

140

But there were three of them, and this was only one girl they had to face. And no matter what her reputation was, they were sure there wasn't no girl who was better than a man with a gun—let alone three men. Both Booker and Anderson were convinced Slade could take her, and they were just there to back his play. And get paid.

"You boys got the plan in your heads?" Slade asked.

"Yeah," Booker said, "I stand on your right, and Ted on your left."

"You do all the talkin'," Anderson added.

"That's right," Slade said, "and nobody draws until I do."

"We got it, Al," Booker said.

Chapter Thirty-Three

Two hours and five minutes after Morgan Earp saw Buck Fly drive his team down Allen Street, Roxy Doyle presented herself at the front door of the Fly Boarding House. She knocked on the door and it was opened by Mollie fly.

"I'm sorry, Mollie," Roxy said. "I know I should wait, but—"

Mollie reached out and took hold of Roxy's left arm. "It's all right," she said. "We've been expecting you. Come in."

Mollie rushed Roxy in, and then led her to the living room, where a man was seated, drinking coffee. He had the look of someone fresh from a bathtub. His hair was still wet.

"Roxy, this is my husband, Buck."

Buck stood up, smiled and extended his hand.

"Glad to meet you," he said, as they shook.

"No, it's me who's glad to meet you, Mr. Fly."

"Oh, just call me Buck."

"All right, Buck."

"Have a seat," Buck said.

"Coffee, Roxy?"

"No, thanks. I've been drinking coffee for the past hour."

"Something stronger?" she offered.

"No. I'd just like to talk."

Mollie looked at Buck, who shrugged. She sat down next to him on the sofa.

"Okay," he said to Roxy, "let's talk."

"I'm sure Mollie's told you who I am."

"You're Roxy Doyle, known as Lady Gunsmith, the daughter of Gavin Doyle. That's what I've been told."

"I don't know how to prove it to you."

"Forget that. If the Earps believe you, I believe you."

"Okay, thank you for that," she said. "Recently, I saw a photo you took of my father, a portrait."

"Where did you see it?"

"In Santa Fe, at the Mathew Brady Gallery."

"That phony, Benson!" he said, with distaste.

"Well, I got him to tell me who actually took the picture, and that's why I'm here."

"What do you think I can tell you?" Fly asked.

"First, when did you take that picture?"

"Oh . . . probably six months ago."

Roxy's heart sank. If it had been that long ago, how could Fly give her any indication as to where her father might be. The best he'd be able to do was tell her where he went when he left Tombstone.

So she asked him.

"I don't have any idea."

"Well, what did you talk about?"

"Nothing," he said. "He didn't talk. Look, I saw him in town and asked if I could take his picture. I didn't even know who he was until he was in my gallery, posing."

"Then why did you want to photograph him?"

"He had that kind of face," Fly said. "I had to capture it before it changed. They do you know. Change. Faces, I mean."

143

"Well, sure, as we get older," Roxy said.

"As we live," Fly said. "Life makes all the changes."

"Okay," Roxy said, not wanting to argue about what caused the most changes to somebody's face. "So, he didn't give you any indication where he might be going when he left here?"

"No," Fly said. "He told me he was a bounty hunter, but at that time he wasn't workin'."

"Then what was he doing here?"

"Actually," Fly said, "he did say somethin'. He said he was tryin' to stay out of trouble."

"Well," Roxy said, "at least we have that in common."

"I'm sorry I can't tell you more," Fly said. "He posed for me, and then he left without even seeing the photograph."

"The next day?"

"The same day. He walked out of the gallery, got on his horse, and rode out of town."

"Did he talk to anybody else while he was here?" Roxy asked. "The Earps, Doc Holliday? Anyone?"

"As I remember," Fly said, "The Marshal had gone to Bisbee, along with Wyatt and Morgan."

"And Doc?"

"I don't know," he said. "You'll have to ask him."

"I've talked with Doc," Roxy said. "I'd think he would have mentioned something like that to me."

"I don't know Doc real well," Fly said, "but I get the feelin' he says what he wants, when he wants to."

"That's probably true."

"Besides," Fly said, "you just might have to ask him."

"Well," Roxy said, standing, "if you can't tell me anything else, maybe that's what my next step will be."

Fly stood.

"I'm sorry I wasn't more helpful."

Mollie stood.

"I'll walk you to the door."

***

"What the hell is she doin' in there?" Anderson asked, again.

"That's the third time, Ted," Booker said. "Give it a rest."

"Why didn't we just take her outside the Bird Cafe," he said. "I thought that's what we were doin' there."

"I had second thoughts," Slade said. "Shootin' there would have brought Wyatt Earp and Doc Holliday out into the street. Here, who's gonna come runnin'? A photographer and his wife. No, this is better."

"It's takin' longer, though," Anderson said.

"Why are you in so much of a hurry to kill this woman?" Booker asked.

"I just don't like the idea of killin' a woman," Anderson admitted. "So I wanna get it over with."

"And get paid, right?" Slade asked.

"Well, yea, get paid," Anderson said.

"Then shut up and wait," Slade said, "and it'll be worth it in the end."

"Yeah, worth it to you," Anderson said. "You're gonna have a big rep after this."

"A bigger rep, Ted," Slade said, "a bigger reputation than I already have. In a town like this, that's important."

"The front door's openin'!" Anderson hissed.

Chapter Thirty-Four

When Roxy stepped out the door she saw them, immediately. So did Mollie.

"What's this?"

"Go back inside, Mollie," Roxy said. "Don't come out until it's over."

"Until what's over?"

Roxy looked at her.

"Oh." Mollie went back inside.

Roxy turned to face the three men in the street.

"You gents waiting for someone?" she asked.

"Yeah," the one in the middle said, "we're waitin' on you, Lady Gunsmith. That's who you are, ain't it?"

"To some people."

"Well," he said, "that's who you are to us."

She studied the three of them. The one in the center had the most confidence. He was looking right at her. The two men on either side of him—while roughly the same age—had none of his swagger. They were standing nervously and paying attention to his every move. When he drew, they would, too. So she had to concentrate on him, first. Take care of him and the other two would probably bolt.

"Well, do I get to come down there?" she asked.

"Right where you are is just fine," the spokesman said.

"What's your name?"

"Why do you care?"

"I'd like to know the name of the man who's killing me," she said, "or who I'm going to kill."

"Well, lady, my name's Slade, Alex Slade, if that makes you feel any better."

"It doesn't," she said, and drew. She went first because what these men were going to do was obvious, and she didn't have time to waste.

She fired once and punched a hole right in his chest before he could react. His eyes went wide and he fell over backwards, his gun still in his holster.

The other two both stopped with their hands halfway to their guns.

"Let's call it finished?" she suggested, holstering her weapon.

Both men stared at her, still crouched in a ready position, and then one of them said, "Aw, we don't get paid if we don't try."

"Damn it—" the other one said, and they both went for their guns.

Roxy drew and fired twice, and they joined their colleague on their backs, dead in the street.

"That's what I say," she agreed, ejecting her spent cartridges and then reloading and holstering the gun. "Damn it."

Chapter Thirty-Five

She didn't notice the flashes of light from behind her until there was another. She turned and looked and saw Fly on the porch, with his camera set up. He had just taken a photo of the three dead men and he had probably taken a few others before it.

"Buck—"

"Sorry," he said, "but when Mollie told me what was happening . . . it was just instinct, you know?"

"Yes," she said, because she knew all about instinct, "I know. Where's Mollie?"

"I sent her out the back to fetch the Marshal."

"That's good."

She turned and they both looked again at the dead men. Then she stepped into the street and, just to make sure, bent over to check them.

Dead.

"That was somethin'!" Fly said.

"Yeah," she said, "something stupid."

"Well, once they were committed they had to go on with it" he said. "That's men."

"That's stupid," Roxy said. "They could have walked away and stayed alive."

"Would you like to wait inside for Marshal Earp?" Fly offered.

"No," she said. "I'm fine out here."

"I'll wait out here with you, then."

"And no more photographs?" she asked.

"No more photographs," he promised.

***

Moments later Mollie reappeared with Marshal Virgil Earp behind her.

"So it happened," he said. It wasn't a question.

"It did," Roxy said. "They tried for me as soon as I came out the door. Are these Clanton's men?"

Virgil studied their faces.

"They're not part of the Cowboys," he said. "So he might have brought them in from out of town."

"So you don't know them at all?"

"This one," he said, touching the center one with the toe of his boot, "is Slade, a would-be gunny."

"His mouth was faster than his gun hand," Roxy announced.

"Figures," Virgil said. "That was always the way I had him pegged."

Virgil took the time to collect some "volunteers" to remove the bodies from in front of the Fly's boarding house, then sat on the front steps next to Roxy. The Flys had gone back inside.

"You talk to Buck?"

"I did."

"Did he help you with anythin' about your father?"

"No," she said. "He just said that when he was here he wasn't working. He sat for the photograph, and then left town immediately."

"Did he tell you when he was here?"

"Seems it was about the time when you and your brother Wyatt were in Bisbee."

"I remember that," he said. "But Morgan was still here."

"And Doc?"

"Yeah, Doc was here, too."

"Do you know if Morgan or Doc talked to my father?"

"Neither of them said anythin' about Gavin Doyle when Wyatt and I got back," Virgil said. "But you can ask them."

"I will."

"How much longer will you be stayin'?" he asked.

"A day or two," she said. "No more. Do you think Clanton will try again?"

"Oh yeah," Virgil said. "Unless . . ."

"Unless what?"

"Unless you want to go and talk to him, tell him you're not takin' sides," Virgil said, "and that you'll be leavin' Tombstone soon."

Roxy thought a moment, then said, "I could do that. But could I do it without him trying to kill me the moment he sees me?"

"I can take you to see him," Virgil offered.

"Will he try to kill you the minute he sees you?" she asked.

"No," Virgil said, "he's not ready for that just yet. That would cause an all out war between the Cowboys and Earps. Just let me know if you want to do that, and I'll take you."

Virgil stood up, put his hand out to help Roxy get to her feet.

"Thank you," she said. "You're a gentleman."

"I have to go to the undertaker about those bodies, try to identify the other two," he said. "Can I walk you somewhere?"

"I'll just tag along back to Allen Street," she said. "Then I'll go to the Bird Cage to talk to Doc and Wyatt about my dad. Hopefully, one of them did have a conversation with him, and it might be helpful."

"I sure hope, for your sake, Roxy, that's true," Virgil said.

Chapter Thirty-Six

Roxy entered the Bird Cage, found that conversation was going to be difficult as there was now a show going on. Girls were dancing around the stage while the piano played, and men were in the balconies cheering them on. At the same time the games were still going on, both poker and Faro. She also noticed right away that Wyatt wasn't dealing at the Faro table, and Doc wasn't playing poker.

She went to the bar, where the bartender was watching the show with a big grin on his face. When he saw her he came over, but didn't lose the grin.

"Beer?" he yelled.

"No," she said, "Wyatt and Doc. Will they be back?"

"Probably," he said, loudly, "they stepped out to get a steak."

At that point Roxy realized she was hungry.

"Do you know where they went?"

"Sure," he said, "where they usually go. The Crystal Palace."

"Thank you."

She left heading for the Palace.

***

It would be no hardship for her to eat at the Crystal Palace Saloon and Steakhouse, since she liked the food there. As she entered she immediately saw where Wyatt and Doc were seated, together, and walked over.

"I'm sorry to interrupt," she said. "If you're talking about something important—"

"Not at all, dear lady," Doc assured her. "As a matter of fact, have a seat and join us."

"Yes," Wyatt said, "sit. We're still waiting for our steaks, it's no hardship to order one more. Interested?"

"Very," she said.

Doc stood and held her chair for her. Moving quickly for a slightly built, ill man.

"Thank you."

Wyatt waved to the waiter and, through hand motions, ordered another steak dinner. The middle-aged waiter nodded that he understood.

"What brings you here?" Doc asked. "I assume you were lookin' for us? Or one of us?"

"Actually," she said, "I was looking for you, Doc."

"Lucky man!" Wyatt said, with a grin.

"What can I do for the Lady Gunsmith?" Doc asked.

"Well, first, don't call me that," she said.

"Now you sound like Clint," Wyatt said. "Never likes to be called the Gunsmith to his face."

"Well, he has a name and so do I," she said. "Just call me Roxy, please."

"Very well. Roxy," Doc said. "What can I do for you?"

"Doc, Buck Fly told me you were in town when my father was here."

"And when was that?" Wyatt asked.

154

"While you and Virgil were in Bisbee."

"Ah," Wyatt said, "that counts me out, then." He sat back, as if to just watch and listen.

"We're talkin' about Gavin Doyle, right?" Doc asked.

"That's right."

"When was that?" Doc asked Wyatt. "Five, six months ago?"

"Six, I think."

Doc looked at Roxy.

"I think if I had talked to Gavin Doyle six months ago I'd remember," he said.

"So you didn't?"

"'fraid not," Doc said. "I sure wish I could be more helpful."

Roxy looked at Wyatt and was about to speak when the waiter appeared with three steak dinners.

"Here ya go, folks," he said, doling them out. "Enjoy."

Each plate was practically taken up by the steak, with vegetables tucked in all the spaces around it, and onions smothering them.

"Why don't we eat," Wyatt suggested, "and then we can continue the conversation."

"Agreed," Roxy said, picking up her fork and steak knife. "I'm starving!"

* * *

They all ate voraciously and waited until they had coffee and slices of pie in front of them to continue the conversation.

"Can I tell you anything else, Roxy?" Doc asked.

"I don't think so, Doc, but Wyatt, maybe you can."

"How? We've already established that I wasn't even here. And I've never met Gavin Doyle."

"That's right, you weren't here," she said, "but Buck Fly told me Morgan was."

"I remember," Virgil said. "I left Morgan here, in charge, because he's my deputy, and asked Wyatt to come with me to Bisbee to pick up a prisoner."

"Do you think Morgan might have talked with my father? Maybe in the line of duty as a deputy?"

"Now," Wyatt said, "that's possible. He's probably over at the office right now. We could go and ask him."

"Oh, I can do that—" Roxy started.

"Nonsense!" Doc scoffed at the idea. "We'll walk you over there."

"Then you should know something before we walk," she said. "Do either of you know a man named Slade?"

"A would-be gunfighter," Doc said, "but he doesn't have the talent for it. Why?"

"He and two other men tried to kill me earlier this evening, as I came out of the Fly boarding house."

"And?" Wyatt asked. "What happened?"

"Well . . . they didn't succeed."

"What happened to them?" Doc asked.

"Oh, they're dead."

"All three?" Doc asked.

"All three."

The two exchanged a glance.

"I wanted you to know," she went on, "just in case there's somebody else out there waiting to take a shot. I don't want either of you getting hit by a stray bullet."

"Don't worry, Roxy," Wyatt said. "If Doc or I get hit by a bullet in Tombstone, you can bet your boots it won't be a stray."

Chapter Thirty-Seven

Roxy walked with Wyatt Earp to the marshal's office, while Doc Holliday headed back to the Bird Cage. When they got there Morgan was seated at the desk, with his feet up on it. When he saw Wyatt he dropped his feet to the ground, hastily.

"Morg, the lady's got somethin' to ask you, and I'm gonna leave you two alone to talk about it." He touched the brim of his hat. "Roxy."

"Thanks, Wyatt."

"Have a seat," Morgan said. "What can I do for you?"

She went through her story again, about Bisbee and her father being in Tombstone.

Morgan scratched the beard stubble on his face as he thought.

"Six months ago?"

Roxy didn't see why the length of time would have anything to do with it. If any of these men had talked with Gavin Doyle, they'd remember. It wasn't every day a man with a reputation like that came to town. Although, there *were* plenty of reputations in Tombstone to begin with. It was probably the same when Dodge City and Abilene were wild towns. Who'd notice one more reputation?

"Can't say as I recollect talkin' with a man like Gavin Doyle. I'd remember somethin' like that."

"Really?" she asked. "His reputation wouldn't get lost in this town?"

"Gavin Doyle? Not likely. As lawmen Virgil and me, we'd have to talk with him when he rode in—if we recognized him."

"So he came to town without anybody knowing he was here, except for Buck Fly?"

"I guess so," Morgan said.

Roxy now wondered if all the men were telling her the truth. How could a bounty hunter like her father go unnoticed, even in a town like Tombstone?

"Well, I guess that's it, then," she said, preparing to leave.

"I'm sorry I couldn't help you more," Morgan said.

"Yeah, thanks. That's what everyone's telling me."

Morgan seemed to be at a loss for words as she walked out of the marshal's office, less than satisfied with her visit to Tombstone.

She headed off down the street, without knowing where she was going next. She couldn't think of any reason why the men in town would want to lie to her about her father, but nevertheless, she had a feeling someone was.

But who?

***

Roxy decided to stay away from the Bird Cage for the rest of the night. Then something occurred to her. If her father *was* in Tombstone working, who was he more likely to be hunting down?

She didn't know where Virgil would be at this time, probably out making his rounds, but it seemed a pretty safe bet that at one time or another, he'd stop in the Bird Cage. She decided to take up a position across the street from the front of the Cage and simply wait for Virgil to put in an appearance. Luckily, there was some chairs on the boardwalk, so she pulled one over and got comfortable.

***

"She what?" Ike Clanton asked his brother, Billy

"She killed 'em, Ike."

"All three?"

Billy nodded.

"All three," he said. "Just like that, lickety-split."

"So maybe she is as good as they say," Curly Bill Brocius spoke up.

"First of all," Ike replied, "ain't nobody as good as they say she is. Second, those three boys weren't even second rate. I just thought Slade would be able to handle a girl."

"So what are we gonna do now?" Billy asked.

Ike looked up at his brother and said, "Siddown and have a beer, kid. I got some thinkin' to do."

"Want me to help. Ike?" Curly Bill asked, from the bar.

"You just sit tight, Curly Bill. I'll tell ya when I need ya."

"Just so's you know, Ike," Curly Bill said. "I can handle a girl."

"Right. I'll keep that in mind."

***

It was starting to get dark when Virgil Earp appeared, walking up Allen Street toward the Bird Cage. Roxy got out of her chair and crossed the street quickly, to intercept him.

"I want to take you up on your offer, Marshal," she told him.

"What offer was that, Roxy?"

"I'd like to go and see Ike Clanton."

"Why the change of heart?"

"It just occurred to me that the man my dad might have talked to when he came to town was Ike Clanton. I mean, if he was working, and looking for a man with a price on his head, wouldn't it be likely that a man like that would be working for Clanton?"

"I reckon it would, at that."

"So when can we go?"

"No time like the present, I guess," Virgil said. "Ike usually spends time in some of the smaller, dirtier saloons in town. We'll just have to go trollin' for him."

"Well," she said, "I'm ready to troll."

Chapter Thirty-Eight

They went to three of Tombstone's smaller, dirtiest saloons until they finally located Ike Clanton and his men in one called The Bucket of Blood.

As they peered in over the batwing doors Virgil said, "Ike's sittin' at that table with his brother, Billy. At the bar is Curly Bill Brocius, one of his men."

"No sign of Ringo?"

"Ringo has better taste than to be in a place like this, unless Ike called for him." He looked at her. "Are you ready?"

"I reckon I'm as ready as I'll ever be," she said. "I've already killed three men, today. What's a few more, if it comes to it?"

"Well, let's try and keep it down to a minimum," Virgil suggested, and pushed in the doors.

***

Ike immediately saw Marshal Virgil Earp enter the saloon, without his brothers and without Doc Holliday. If Ike wanted him dead, he'd be dead in a minute, except for one thing. The person Virgil had with him.

This redhaired, busty woman with a gun on her hip had to be Lady Gunsmith, Roxy Doyle. Now the question was, what the hell were these two doing here?

***

Roxy saw Ike Clanton looking at her as she and Virgil approached his table. He had the eyes of a wolf, a killer wolf, and they were fixed on her.

"Well, Marshal Earp," Clanton said, "what brings you here?"

At the sound of Virgil's name Ike's brother, Billy, turned to look. The minute he saw Roxy standing next to Virgil, Roxy could see he only had eyes for her. And he couldn't have been more than 18 or 19. Maybe later she'd be able to use this to her advantage.

She also saw Curly Bill push off the bar, stand up straight, with his hand down by his gun.

"You better calm your dogs, Mr. Clanton," she said.

Ike looked over at the bar and said, "Relax, Billy. I get the feelin' these two are here to talk." He looked at Virgil and Roxy. "Is that right?"

"It is," Virgil said. "This lady is—"

"You don't have to introduce the Lady Gunsmith to me, Virgil," Ike said.

"Well, she has somethin' she wants to ask you, Ike," Virgil said. "I told her you'd be a gentleman and listen."

Curly Bill started to laugh at that at the bar, but he stopped when Ike gave him a hard look.

"What's the question, Miss?" Ike asked.

"I want to know if you spoke to my father when he was in Tombstone six months ago."

"Your father?"

She nodded.

"Gavin Doyle."

"The bounty hunter?" he asked. "That's who your father is?"

"Yes."

Ike sat back in his chair.

"Ike, wasn't that the fella—" Billy started, but Ike cut him off sharply.

"Shut up, Billy!"

Billy quieted down, turned to look at Roxy, again. She gave him a smile, knowing it would get him going even more.

"What makes you think your father would've come to talk to me?" Ike asked her.

"He's a bounty hunter," she said. "It's his business to hunt trash like you."

Ike jerked as if he had been slapped.

"Listen, bitch—" Ike started.

"Easy, Ike," Virgil said. "Remember what I said about bein' a gentleman."

"I ain't no gentleman and we both know it, Marshal," Ike said. "As for you, missy, I never saw your father, six months ago or any other time. So you better be on your way before I sic my dogs on you."

Curly Bill pushed away from the bar, again.

"Relax, Ike," Virgil said. "we're goin'."

He turned to leave, but Roxy took a moment to lock eyes with young Billy before she turned and followed the lawman.

Outside Virgil said, "I'm sorry about that."

"Don't worry yourself about it, Virgil," she said. "I've heard worse."

"You want to come to the Bird Cage for a drink?"

"No, I'm going to stay around here, a while."

"What for?"

"I think there was somebody in that saloon who wants to talk to me."

"Curly Bill?" he asked. "I don't think he wants to talk to you."

"Not Curly Bill," Roxy said. "The kid, Billy. Did you see the way he was looking at me?"

"You mean like a lovesick cow?"

"That's how I mean," she said. "And Ike had to shut him up before he said something."

"So you figure Billy knows somethin'."

"I do," she said, "and I'm going to find out what it is."

"Well, be careful," Virgil said. "He may be a kid, but he's still a Clanton."

"I will, Virgil," she said. "Thanks for your help."

"I'll see you later, then," he said, turning and walking off toward Allen Street.

Chapter Thirty-Nine

Roxy had to wait over an hour, and by then darkness had fallen, completely. This was not a well-travelled part of town, so there were no street lights. She was going to have to depend on the light emanating from the saloon, and the moon.

Finally, the batwing doors swung open and Billy Clanton came walking out. He was a bit unsteady, since he had been drinking. He started off down the street and she stayed with him, while remaining on the other side. She needed a likely place to pull him aside, and that probably meant an alley.

They walked that way to a better lit section of town, and she finally spotted her chance. He was coming up on an alley, so she started across.

"Billy!"

He turned at the sound of his name and looked surprised to see her coming toward him.

"What do you want?" he demanded, his hand going toward his gun.

"Relax," she said, coming up on him. "I just want to talk."

"About what?"

"Well, for one thing, about how handsome you are."

He relaxed noticeably.

"Really?"

"Definitely," she said, rubbing his left arm. "Is there somewhere we could be alone? How about this alley?"

"Huh? Oh, uh, sure."

She linked her arm into his and led him into the alley. He was a few inches shorter than she was, and it seemed like more than six years to her since she had been about his age. At 25, she'd been feeling a lot older, of late.

"There," she said, turning him to face her. "Now we're alone." She leaned in and kissed him. She could tell he wasn't very experienced, but eventually he started reacting eagerly, and that was when she pulled away.

"Well, she said, "I've been wanting to do that since I first saw you."

"Oh my God," he said, "me, too. You're so beautiful!"

"Why, thank you."

"Can we do that again?" he asked.

"Sure."

She kissed him again, this time pressing him back against the side of the building and sliding her hand down the front of his jeans. He had an impressive bulge there, and she massaged it through the denim.

"Oh, God!" he gasped. She kept her hand pressed to his crotch.

"Wow," she said. "That feels impressive."

"Uh, t-thanks."

"Can I see it?"

His eyes widened.

"Right here?"

"Right here," she said, undoing his belt, "right now." She leaned in and kissed him on the ear, and then whispered, "I want it."

She undid the button, slid her hand into his pants, down his belly until she came in contact with his hard cock. She wrapped her hand around it and thought that this might not be so unpleasant.

"Oh my," she said, "yes, that is nice."

"Oh, God!" he said closing his eyes.

She leaned in and put her lips to his ear, again.

"Would you like me to take it out and put it in my mouth, Billy?"

"Jeez, yeah!"

"Mmmm," she hummed, as she undid his gunbelt, let it fall to the ground, then slid his trousers down his thighs until his hard cock popped out. It was really too dark in the alley for her to get a good look at it, unless she got on her knees, and although he was expecting her to do that, she wasn't about to.

Instead, she began to stroke it and said, "But before I do that, Billy, I want to ask you something."

"W-what is it?" he asked.

She continued to stroke his dick, hoping he wouldn't finish before she got her answers.

"When Ike told you to shut up, Billy, what were you going to say?"

"H-huh, W-wha—"

"In the saloon," she went on, "when I asked about my father, you were going to say something, but Ike told you to shut up."

"Uh, Ike's my older b-brother," he stammered.

"So he gets to tell you what to say, and when?" she asked. "A man like you, with a tallywacker like this?" She squeezed and he gasped. "I'd think you wouldn't let any man tell you what to say or do. That you're your own man."

"I-I *am* my own man!" he insisted.

"Well," she whispered in his ear again, "how would you like to be my man?"

"I-I'd like that just fine."

He reached for her breasts, and she slapped his hand away.

She squeezed his cock again ad said, "Well, we're almost there."

"Jesus—he said, squeezing his eyes shut.

"You answer my question," she said, "I'll suck you dry, and then we'll go to bed together . . . naked!"

His eyes opened wide.

"Ike talked to your father, because he was huntin' one of our men!" He said it all in a rush.

"Who?" she asked. "Who was he hunting?"

"A fella named Caswell, Tom Caswell."

"And did he find him?"

"I dunno," he said, "but Caswell disappeared. Ike said he ran off."

"Then what?"

She was pumping his penis so hard that he suddenly grunted and shot a load of jism clear across the alley, to where it almost struck the other wall. She stepped back just in time to avoid it.

"Oh God!" he said, almost slumping to his knees. Then he put his hands on his thighs and bent over to catch his breath.

"What happened, Billy?" she asked. "What happened between Ike and my father?"

"Nothin'," he gasped. "But Ike claims he had Gavin Doyle killed"

Her stomach dropped.

"By who?" she asked. "Who did Ike have kill my father?"

"Ringo," Billy said. "Ike said he had him killed by Johnny Ringo."

"Do you know where Ringo is now?"

"No," he said, "only Ike ever knows—hey!"

As Roxy stormed out of the alley, Billy shouted, "Are we still gonna get naked together?"

Chapter Forty

Roxy needed to find Johnny Ringo.

He hadn't been in the Bucket of Blood with Ike, but according to Billy, Ike was the only one who knew where he was.

She believed everything Billy told her because, face it, she had his essence in her grasp.

She rushed back to the dirty little saloon, but as soon as she entered she saw that Ike, Curly Bill and his other men were gone.

In order to find Ringo, she had to find Ike. An idea occurred to her, but she decided to put it off until the next day. If she found him now, she'd likely kill him. She needed the night to calm down and consider what Ike and Billy had told her. So she headed back to her hotel.

***

She had breakfast alone in the hotel dining room the next day. None of the Earps, nor Doc Holliday appeared.

Overnight she had decided that before she confronted Ike about finding Ringo, she wanted to go back and talk to Buck Fly. If men were lying to her, then why not him?

She walked to the Fly boarding house and knocked on the door.

"Roxy," Mollie greeted as she opened the door. "I'll bet you're here to see Buck, not me."

"That's right."

"Well, he's out back, in the gallery. You can go around. The door shouldn't be locked."

"Thanks, Mollie."

She walked around the house to the door of the gallery, and although Mollie told her the door would be unlocked, she knocked.

"Come in!"

She opened the door and went in.

"Roxy!" Buck said, with a smile. He was standing at a camera mounted on a tripod. "You're just in time."

"For what?"

"To pose."

"Oh, I don't think—"

"Not for real," he said. "I'm trying out a new piece of equipment and I just need a subject to focus on."

"Oh, all right."

"Just sit on that stool, over there," he said, pointing.

She sat down and faced the camera lens.

"That's perfect." He tucked his head underneath the hood. "What brings you here?"

"I have a few more questions for you," she said.

"Well, go ahead," he said. "I can work and talk at the same time."

"Did you lie to me, Buck?"

There was a moment of hesitation, and then he came out from beneath the hood.

"About what?" he asked.

"My father," she said. "The word I got from someone last night was that he was hunting a man named Caswell."

"If he was he didn't mention the name to me," the photographer said. He went back under the hood. "Can you raise your chin just a bit?"

She did so.

"Great. So who told you this?"

"Billy Clanton."

"And you believed him?"

"I had him in a position where he had to tell me the truth," she said.

He came out from beneath the hood again and frowned as if trying to remember.

"Caswell. No, your father never mentioned him, or anyone, for that matter. We didn't talk about the Earps, the Clantons, Doc Holliday—you know, I thought it was kind of odd, at the time."

"Why's that?"

"Well," he said, "who comes to Tombstone and doesn't talk about them?"

"I don't know," she said. "Maybe somebody who's trying to lie low."

"He didn't say anythin' about that, either," Fly said. "Layin' low, I mean."

Roxy got off the stool.

"I'll have to ask Ike, then," Roxy said.

"Won't that be dangerous?"

"Not as dangerous as when I talk to Johnny Ringo."

"Sounds like you better have the law with you," Fly said, "either Marshal Earp, or Sheriff Behan."

"You know," Roxy said. "I haven't talked to Sheriff Behan about this, at all. Thanks for the suggestion, Buck."

"One more thing, Roxy," he said, as she started for the door.

"What's that?"

"Can you give me the address of that Mathew Brady Gallery?" he asked. "I've got to get to that bastard Benson."

"Why?" she asked.

"It's that photo of your dad," Buck said.

"What about it?"

"Well," Buck Fly said, "the truth is, he stole it!"

"Why would he do that?" she asked.

"I'll ask him when I see him," he said. "If you'll tell me where to find him, I'll go and get it back."

"I can do that." She told him about the gallery in Santa Fe, and exactly where it was.

"Thank you, Roxy," he said. "Now, I've got one more request, before you go."

"What's that?"

"I'd like to photograph you for real," he said. "I mean, since I did your father I thought, maybe . . .?"

She hesitated, unsure, but then he went further, and she knew what her answer was.

"And I'd like you to be . . . nude." He rushed on. "It would be very artistic, very tasteful—"

Since she knew what had happened the last time she posed nude, and what it led to she said, "I'm afraid not, Buck. And what would Mollie think?"

He rubbed his hands together.

"Mollie wouldn't have to know."

She turned and left, her opinion of Buck Fly completely changed.

Chapter Forty-One

Sheriff Johnny Began looked up in surprise as Roxy Doyle entered his office.

"Well, Lady Gunsmith," he said, sitting back in his chair. "What brings me this kind of luck?"

"I'm looking for somebody who might have talked to my father when he was in town six months ago."

"And you think I did?"

"You're the sheriff," she said. "Don't you talk to strangers when they ride in?"

"I do," Behan said. "but I never saw him."

"That's funny," Roxy said, "I heard my father was here looking for a man named Caswell, who worked for Ike Clanton."

"Caswell," Behan repeated, then shook his head. "No, never heard of him."

"I also heard that Johnny Ringo might have killed my father."

"Stories have been going around for years about Gavin Doyle dying or being killed. What makes you think this one is true?"

"I think I'd like to ask Ringo, myself."

"Alone?"

"Unless you want to take me to him?"

Behan put his hands in the pockets of the vest of his three piece suit and stared at her for a few moments.

"And what's in it for me if I do?"

"What do you want?" she asked.

"Well, he said, "we could start with supper together."

"Fine," she said, "you take me to Johnny Ringo and we'll have supper together."

"If he doesn't kill us."

"Right."

He studied her again, then took his hands out of his pockets and stood up. "All right. Come on."

***

When they reached the front of the Bucket of Blood, Roxy asked, "Why are we here?"

"You want Ringo, right?"

"That's right."

"Well, Ike's the one who can get him to see you."

"And Ike is in the saloon this early?"

"Usually."

They mounted the boardwalk and entered, Roxy wondering if she was letting Behan walk her into a trap.

Ike was at the same table as when she came with Virgil.

"Let me guess," Ike said to Behan. "Now she's got you under her thumb?"

"Not exactly," Behan said. "We've come to an understanding."

"And what does that have to do with me?"

"Not you," Behan said. "Ringo."

"Johnny?" Ike looked at Roxy. "You got lucky with Ringo once. Next time he'll kill you."

"I just want to talk to him," she said.

"About your father?"

She nodded.

"He's the only one I haven't spoken to," she said. "After that, I'll be on my way."

"That's good news," Ike said.

"So?" Behan asked. "Where is he?"

"You know Ringo," Ike said, "he's either off killin' or fuckin'."

"Well, seems somebody told her Ringo might've killed him."

Ike looked around the room, but his eye didn't fall on the one he wanted. Roxy had the feeling he was looking for his brother Billy. At the bar, Curly Bill Brocius was drinking his breakfast, along with Buckskin Frank Leslie and the McLaury brothers, Tom and Frank.

"Where's your brother, Ike?" Roxy asked. "Where's little Billy?"

Ike looked at her.

"I was just wonderin' the same thing."

"So you're not going to help her find Ringo?" Behan asked.

"You got an arrangement with 'er, you find him for her," Ike said.

"Sorry to have bothered you, Ike," Behan said.

He turned to leave and Roxy followed him.

Ike beckoned to the McLaury boys to come over to his table.

"You," he said, pointing at Tom, "get me Ringo, and you," pointing at Frank, "find Billy."

"Right," they both said.

As they started for the batwing door, he shouted, "Go out the back!"

Curly Bill came over and asked, "You got anythin' you want me to do, Ike?"

Ike gave him a sour look, and then said, "Yeah, get me another beer."

As Curly Bill went to the bar Ike waved Buckskin Frank Leslie over.

"Yeah?"

"Can you take 'er?" Ike asked.

"Probably."

Ike thought a moment.

"I don't wanna risk it," he said. "I might need you later for the Earps."

"So whataya wanna do?" Leslie asked.

Find me Apple Jack Cannon."

Chapter Forty-Two

Outside the Bucket of Blood Behan said, "Sorry, I guess that means no supper."

"You don't have any other ideas?" she asked.

Johnny Behan looked her up and down and said, "Oh, I've got other ideas."

"I mean about finding Johnny Ringo."

"'fraid not," Behan said. "Sorry."

"What if there *was* more in it for you?"

"What are you saying?" he asked. "You'd go to bed with me to get to Johnny Ringo?"

Roxy studied him, and then said. "Nah, never mind. I don't have time to be that bored. I'll find somebody else to help me find him."

He laughed. "Like who? Marshal Virgil Earp?"

"No, I don't think I'll involve the law in this," she said. "But I understand Doc Holliday has had some problems with Johnny Ringo in the past. Maybe he'd like to help me."

"Miss Doyle," Behan said, "you'll be asking for trouble if you hitch your wagon to Doc Holliday. I can guarantee you that."

"Well, maybe that's finally what I'm doing in Tombstone, Sheriff," she said. "Maybe now I'm finally looking for trouble."

She turned and walked away, leaving him standing alone in front of the Bucket of Blood.

***

It was too early for the Bird Cage. Unlike the Bucket of Blood, they didn't open their doors at dawn for men to start drinking and gambling.

She knew Doc had a room in the same place she did, the Grand Hotel, so she decided to start there.

As usual, the hotel desk clerk was delighted to see Roxy. He loved watching her walk towards him and walk away from him.

"Has Doc Holliday come down from his room, this morning?" she asked him.

"Yes, Ma'am," he said.

"Is he in the dining room?"

"No, Ma'am," the clerk said. "He went right out the front door."

"And he didn't say where he was going?"

"No, Ma'am" the clerk said, "but if I may . . ."

"Yeah?"

"You can usually find Doc where you find Wyatt Earp."

"And I suppose Wyatt came down from his room?"

"Yes, Ma'am, and he went right out the front door."

"Okay, thanks."

She walked out of the hotel, conscious of the clerk's stare on her backside.

***

The likeliest place for Wyatt and Doc to be having breakfast was the Crystal Palace. It was where everybody who wanted a decent meal seemed to end up, at one time or another.

She thought about going to the marshal's office, but that would only lead to either Virgil or Morgan, and she didn't want to involve either one of them.

One look inside the door of the Crystal Palace told her that Wyatt and Doc weren't there. She wondered if Ike would be warning Ringo that she was looking for him? A man with his reputation would not be caught dead hiding from a woman. Maybe all she had to do was wait out in the open.

***

But it wasn't Ike Clanton who told Ringo that Roxy was looking for him. It was Billy, the night before, after he had pulled up his pants and left the alley. He had found the gunman in a saloon called The Cattle Queen, playing poker, and had pulled him aside.

"And how did she hear I killed Gavin Doyle?" Ringo asked.

"Um, I mighta told 'er," Billy mumbled.

"And why would you tell her that?"

Billy shrugged.

"I thought she liked me."

"Well, thanks a lot for that, Billy," Ringo said. "Did you tell Ike?"

"No."

"You better not," the gunfighter said. "Your own brother might kill ya."

"You ain't gonna kill me, are ya, Johnny?"

"I might."

"Well, there's no way she can outdraw ya, is there?"

Ringo thought about the first day he'd run into her.

"Not in a fair fight, no," Ringo said.

"So are you gonna face 'er?"

"I don't know what I'm gonna do, Billy," Ringo said, "but I tell you what you oughtta do. Get outta sight and stay there until this is all over, because one of us—Ike or me—might still kill you."

***

That was the night before, and Billy hadn't been seen all day.

Ringo was wondering how to play it, but while he was doing that, Ike looked up from his table in the Bucket of Blood and saw Applejack Cannon walk in.

"You lookin' fer me?" Jack asked.

Apple Jack Cannon was everything Alex Slade had wanted to be, a respected man with a gun who had earned that respect by killing. He wasn't part of Ike Clanton's crew, but he was for hire.

"You heard of Lady Gunsmith?"

"I heard stories," the big man said. In his 40's, no one judged Apple Jack by his appearance, because he didn't look like a fast gun, he looked like a boxer. With fingers the size of sausages you'd never think he could even fire a gun, let alone do it quickly and accurately.

"Well, she's real," Ike assured him, "and she's here, and I want her dead."

Apple Jack sat across from Ike.

"So let's talk money."

Chapter Forty-Three

Roxy was crossing the street after leaving the Crystal Palace and saw six men walking toward her in the street. She also noticed there were no horses or wagons nearby. Seems everybody knew ahead of time that trouble was coming, except her. But that was fine. One of the first things Clint Adams taught her was that with a reputation came the possibility of trouble every time you walk down the street. His advice: just always be ready.

***

Apple Jack Cannon had worked out a price with Ike Clanton that enabled him to recruit five other guns, who were also excited by the possibility of being one of the men to kill Lady Gunsmith. Finding her in the morning wasn't a problem. All he had to do was check all the places that served breakfast. Which was how Apple Jack and his men found her out in front of the Crystal Palace.

But somebody else had the same idea.

***

Johnny Ringo decided that morning to go looking for Roxy Doyle. He knew she was staying in the Grand Hotel, but he also knew Wyatt and Doc were there. If he ran into Doc

Holliday tempers were going to flare, because they always did between the two of them. He wasn't sure what it was he disliked about Doc, or what it was Doc hated about him, but it was there. They'd been putting it aside for a long time, eventually it was going to come to a head.

But maybe not today.

He entered the hotel lobby and asked the desk clerk if he'd seen Lady Gunsmith that morning.

"Yessir, Mr. Ringo," the clerk said. "She's been out, and in, and out again."

"Do you know where she went?"

"She's, uh, looking for Mr. Earp and Mr. Holliday, I, uh, believe."

"Okay," Ringo said, and left.

He knew the Bird Cage would be closed this early, so he headed for the Crystal Palace.

***

Roxy did the only thing she could do, because the alternative was to run, and she wasn't about to do that.

So she turned to face six men.

***

"Well, lookee there," Apple Jack said. "I thought sure she'd run."

"That's Lady Gunsmith," his partner, Hal Frederick said. Apple Jack and Hal had been riding together for ten years.

When they needed help, they recruited it, which was what they had done with the other four men with them.

"C'mon," Jack said, "you don't believe that shit, do you? A girl who's faster than a man?"

"No," Hal said, "but maybe she does, and if she does then the last thing she'd do is run. That's all I'm sayin'."

Apple Jack shook his head.

"Stupid."

***

Roxy tried to relax as she waited for the men to reach her. She was relieved to see that none of them were Johnny Ringo.

When they reached her, she was able to immediately pick out the leader. She didn't know who he was, but recognized the look, and knew he'd be the one to speak.

And she was right.

"You're Roxy Doyle."

"You think so?"

He smiled, and it wasn't pretty. He was a big, wide man who looked as if he could tear her apart, not outdraw her. But somehow, she doubted he would die as easily as Slade and the others.

"The long, red hair, the gun," he said. "Who else would you be? Wild Bill Hickok?"

"Hickok had nice hair," the man next to him said.

"That's funny, Hal."

The other four men weren't talking, they had just fanned out, and were waiting for the word. Roxy thought Clint Adams

187

might have gotten out of this situation alive, but she doubted she would. One other thing he had taught her early on was that if she went this way, her end would be from a bullet.

This would be a lot of bullets.

Looked like she wasn't going to find her father, after all.

Then she heard steps on the boardwalk behind her, and someone stepped down to stand next to her.

"Hello, Apple Jack," a man said.

"What're you doin' here, Ringo?" the man called Apple Jack asked.

"This just didn't look fair, Jack," Ringo said. "This look fair to you, Miss Doyle?"

"I think so." she said. "I've got them right where I want them."

Johnny Ringo laughed.

"You probably do, at that," he said, "but I couldn't just keep walkin' when I saw what was happenin' here and, make no mistake about it, I ain't even a gentleman. But if you don't mind, I'll just stand right here until it's over, so I have a good seat to see the end."

"Be my guest," she said.

"Okay, Jack," Johnny Ringo said. "carry on."

Chapter Forty-Four

Well, given a guess, Roxy would never have seen herself standing shoulder-to-shoulder in a street fight with Johnny Ringo, but there they were.

The man next to Apple Jack stood solidly, but Roxy noticed the other men shifting their feet nervously at the appearance of Johnny Ringo.

"Tate, that you?" Ringo said to one of them.

"Hello, Johnny," the homely looking man on the end said.

"Never thought I'd find you standing in the street goin' against me with a gun, Tate."

"Wouldn't have been my first choice, Johnny," Tate said. "I didn't know you'd be here."

"So you just hired on to gun down a lone woman, huh?"

Tate looked embarrassed.

"And Steiner, you, too?"

"It's just a job," Charlie Steiner said.

"Yeah, just a job," Ringo said. "Well, I guess we better get on with it." He looked at Roxy. "You wanna let them draw first, or should we just . . ."

"We might as well—" she started to reply, and that's when Apple Jack drew his gun.

He was fast. So fast, in fact, that Roxy was shocked. This Apple Jack, whatever his last name was, was one of the fastest men she'd ever faced.

But he was still moving in slow motion compared to her.

She drew, fired, and two holes appeared in Apple Jack's chest. That's when she realized both she and Ringo had beaten him to the draw, and that both of them had chosen to shoot him, first.

Hal Fredericks didn't hesitate. He wasn't as fast as his partner, though, so while Apple Jack had actually cleared leather by the time he was shot, Hal did not. He joined his partner on the ground, dead.

The other four hired guns—Tate, Steiner and the other two—all hesitated, and paid for it. Roxy shot two, and Ringo the other two.

By the time the echo of the shots had faded, six men were dead in the street.

Then Roxy and Johnny Ringo turned to face each other, each still with two bullets in their hands.

"What now?" Ringo asked.

Roxy holstered her gun. Ringo followed her example. People had come running toward the sound of the shots, but now they stopped short as they saw the two survivors facing each other. Maybe it wasn't over. They froze in the street, and on the boardwalk, to watch.

"The law's gonna be here soon," Ringo said. "Behan or Earp."

"I got the word that you killed my father, Gavin Doyle, six months ago."

"Got it from who? That idiot Billy Clanton?"

"Is it true?"

He stared at her.

"I'm gonna tell you somethin' I ain't told anybody else," he said. "I met your father when he came here, and we talked."

"About what?"

"A man named Caswell."

"So he *was* working when he came here."

"Yeah, he was hunting Caswell."

"And what happened?"

"Caswell heard your father was on his way here to nab him, and he lit out."

"Did you tell my father that?"

"Yes."

"So you didn't kill him?"

"We never even said a cross word to each other," Ringo said. "I told him where Caswell was headed, and that was it."

"Was this before or after he sat for a portrait with Buck Fly?"

"I don't know anything about that," Ringo said. "I'm tellin' you the truth."

"Why?" she asked. "Why are you telling me the truth?"

"Why not?" he asked, with a shrug. "It's better than one of us killin' the other."

"And you're not sure which way that would go?"

He thought back to their first encounter and said, "No, I ain't."

"Fair enough," she said, as Virgil and Morgan Earp both ran up onto the scene.

"What the hell happened here?" Virgil demanded.

"You tell 'em," Ringo said. "They'd never believe me."

Chapter Forty-Five

Roxy and Johnny Ringo waited in the marshal's office while the bodies were removed from the street. Morgan sat with them. They just remained quiet until Virgil came back in.

"Okay," he said, "you've both told your story and it matches. Since I know both Apple Jack and Hal Frederick are guns for hire, I don't have any trouble believing they started it."

"Good."

"What I do have trouble with," Virgil went on, "is understanding why Johnny Ringo would help you."

"Maybe," Roxy said, "he's a gentleman."

"That ain't it," Ringo said.

"Then why?" Virgil asked. "You know Ike sent those jaspers after her. I would've thought you'd be with them."

"I just didn't like the situation, Marshal," Ringo said, standing up. "Don't get the idea I'm switchin' sides. Can I go?"

"Sure, Ringo," Virgil said. "Get outta here."

As he started to leave Roxy stood and grabbed his left arm.

"Thanks, Johnny. And not just for standing with me."

"Sure."

Ringo went out the door.

"Am I free to go, too?" she asked Virgil.

"Yeah, I don't see why not."

She hurried out of the office, looked both ways on the street, spotted Ringo and ran after him.

"Johnny!"

He turned when he heard his name, thinking again of the first time he'd seen her.

"What?"

When she reached him she grabbed his arm, again.

"I'm not going to be around much longer," she said.

"Is that right?"

"I thought maybe you and me could make my last night here . . . memorable."

She'd given this some thought. He was a rough looking man, the kind she found attractive. She was going to be on the trail for a while and might need a little care and comfort before she left Tombstone. The best looking man in town was Sheriff John Behan, but he knew it, which took away from his appeal. The Earps were all married, and Doc Holliday was sickly. That put Johnny Ringo square in her sights—and he'd saved her bacon without being asked, wanting nothing in return.

"You still got your hotel room?" he asked.

"Yes."

"What are we waitin' for?"

***

When the door to her room closed and they were inside *he* grabbed *her* arm, turned her and gathered her up. He was a tall man and she liked the way he cradled her. He kissed her hard, which was what she'd been looking for, and she responded. With her goal in Tombstone achieved, and the shooting done with, she found herself able to enjoy the warmth of him. His taste and feel, the sensations his gunman fingers were sending up and down her spine as he started to undress her left her breathless.

She pulled his shirt open, sending buttons flying across the room, and rubbed her palms over his hairy chest. She didn't usually like hairy men, but for some reason everything about him excited her.

They gravitated toward the bed, and each took a moment to unbuckle their gunbelts and hang them on opposite sides of the bedpost. Then they hurriedly kicked off their boots, shucked their clothes and met in the center of the mattress.

Ringo explored her body with his hands, rubbing and grabbing, but doing so with interest, not with force. She had wondered if he would be a selfish lover, like most men, but that wasn't the case. As he kissed her mouth, neck and shoulders, his hands fondled her breasts, tweaked her nipples, kneaded her flesh, and all of it meant to soothe his desire and bring her pleasure at the same time.

This man was surprising, given his reputation.

As his hands and lips roamed her body she reached down to grasp his long hard cock. That wasn't exactly a surprise, but it was a nice discovery. She stroked him, realizing he had not yet achieved full hardness. By the time he had he felt as if he was going to burst in her hands. She held on tightly and fell onto her back, taking him with her. Then she pulled on him so that the swollen head of his penis was pressing up against the moist lips of her vagina.

"Are you in a hurry?" he asked.

She smiled. "Only the first time."

He plunged into her . . .

***

"You said you told my father where Caswell was going."

"I did."

They had spent the whole night together, then had break-fast. Now they were in front of her hotel, with her horse saddled ready to go.

"Where was that?" she asked. "Where was my father going when he left here?"

"Caswell told me his family had a farm outside of Spring-field, Missouri."

"Missouri?"

"That was the only thing I could tell him," he said. "All I knew."

Her body and mind were now at peace, both thanks to Johnny Ringo—at least, for the moment.

"Thanks, Johnny. You don't know what that means to me."

"When are you leavin' town?" he asked.

"Right away." She looked at her horse, tied to a hitching post, and then back at him. "Why?"

"I'll tell Ike," he said. "He won't have any reason to send anyone else after you, if you leave now."

"I appreciate that," she said. "I'd go after him, but I can't prove he sent those men, and I don't have the time to waste trying. I'm going to leave him to the Earps and Doc Holliday."

They didn't touch. That time had passed. She mounted up and looked down at him.

"When the fuse finally blows, here, Johnny," she said, "I wish you luck."

"Thanks," he said. "Good luck to you, too. I hope you find your father."

***

Weeks later, when she heard about the O.K. Corral, the killing of Morgan Earp, the shooting of Virgil Earp, and then Wyatt Earp's ride for vengeance, she wondered how Johnny Ringo had fared during all of that.

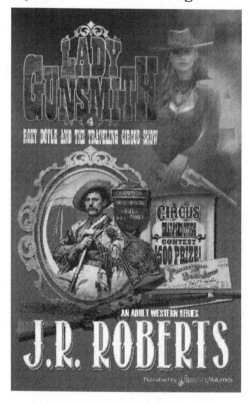

On Sale Now!

Lady Gunsmith 3
Roxy Doyle and The Shanghai Saloon

For more information
visit: www.speakingvolumes.us

On Sale Now!

Lady Gunsmith 2
The Three Graves of Roxy Doyle

For more information
visit:

On Sale Now!

Lady Gunsmith 1
The Legend of Roxy Doyle

For more information
visit: www.speakingvolumes.us

On Sale Now!

THE GUNSMITH *series*
430 - 434
The Show Girl

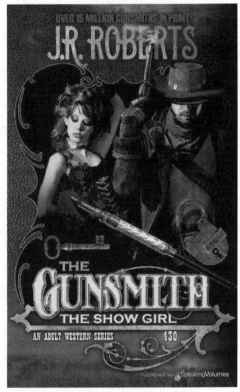

For more information
visit: www.speakingvolumes.us

Made in the USA
San Bernardino, CA
06 August 2019